Megastar Mysteries

Polly

Annabelle Starr

Illustrated by Helen Turner

EGMONT

Special thanks to:

Rennie Brown, St John's Walworth Church of England School
and Belmont Primary School

EGMONT
We bring stories to life

Polly first published in Great Britain 2008
by Egmont UK Limited
239 Kensington High Street, London W8 6SA

Text & illustration © 2008 Egmont UK Ltd
Text by Rennie Brown
Illustrations by Helen Turner

ISBN 978 1 4052 3933 2

1 3 5 7 9 10 8 6 4 2

A CIP catalogue record for this title is available
from the British Library

Typeset by Avon DataSet Ltd, Bidford on Avon, Warwickshire
Printed and bound in Great Britain by the CPI Group

'These books are simply the best! I love trying to solve the mysteries before I get to the end! I love them all!'
Megan, age 10

'I love you Abs, Soph and Rosie and so do my friends'
Jessica, age 10

'*Megastar Mysteries* is the best!'
Rafiah, age 7

'These books are the best I have ever read!'
Zaafirah, age 9

'I think the *Megastar Mysteries* books are great because you have mysteries and girly stuff all in one, and they're so good you can't put them down, so keep writing more please!'
Deirdre, age 10

'These books are brilliant-a-rama! I love them!'
Mary, age 10

We want to know what *you* think about
Megastar Mysteries! Visit:

www.mega-star.co.uk

for loads of coolissimo megastar
stuff to do!

Meet the
Megastar Mysteries Team!

Hello! **Rosie Parker** here, official celebrity magnet and mystery-solver. Meet my best friends . . .

. . . **Soph** (Sophie) **McCoy** – what she can't tell you about fashion just isn't worth knowing – and . . .

. . . **Abs** (Abigail) **Flynn**. She's so clever she should be crowned Brain of Borehurst.

Next up is my mum, **Liz Parker**. Quelle horreur! There must be some serious 1980s freaks out there cos her Bananarama tribute band, the Banana Splits, never seems short of bookings.

And last but not least is my nan, **Pam Parker**. She reckons the key to good sleuthing is a regular diet of murder-mystery TV shows – and, wow, does she digest a lot of those! Not to mention the accompanying biscuits . . .

Consider yourself introduced!

ROSIE'S MINI MEGASTAR PHRASEBOOK

Want to speak our lingo, but don't know your soeurs from your signorinas? No problemo! Just use my comprehensive guide . . .

-a-rama	add this ending to a word to indicate a large quantity: e.g. 'The after-show party was celeb-a-rama'
amigo	Spanish for 'friend'
au contraire, mon frère	French for 'on the contrary, my brother'
au revoir	French for 'goodbye'
barf/barfy/barfissimo	sick/sick-making/very sick-making indeed
bien sûr, ma soeur	French for 'of course, my sister'
bon	French for 'good'
bonjour	French for 'hello'
celeb	short for 'celebrity'
convo	short for 'conversation'
cringe-fest	a highly embarrassing situation
Cringeville	a place we all visit from time to time when something truly embarrassing happens to us
cringeworthy	an embarrassing person, place or thing might be described as this
daggy	Australian for 'unfashionable' or 'unstylish'
doco	short for 'documentary'
exactamundo	not a real foreign word, but a great way to express your agreement with someone
exactement	French for 'exactly'

excusez moi	French for 'excuse me'
fashionista	'a keen follower of fashion' – can be teamed with 'sista' for added rhyming fun
glam	short for 'glamorous'
gorge/gorgey	short for 'gorgeous': e.g. 'the lead singer of that band is gorge/gorgey'
hilarioso	not a foreign word at all, just a great way to liven up 'hilarious'
hola, señora	Spanish for 'hello, missus'
hottie	no, this is *not* short for hot water bottle – it's how you might describe an attractive-looking boy to your friends
-issimo	try adding this ending to English adjectives for extra emphasis: e.g. coolissimo, crazissimo – très funissimo, non?
je ne sais pas	French for 'I don't know'
je voudrais un beau garçon, s'il vous plaît	French for 'I would like an attractive boy, please'
journos	short for 'journalists'
les Français	French for, erm, 'the French'
Loserville	this is where losers live, particularly evil school bully Amanda Hawkins
mais	French for 'but'
marvelloso	not technically a foreign word, just a more exotic version of 'marvellous'
massivo	Italian for 'massive'
mon amie/mes amis	French for 'my friend'/'my friends'
muchos	Spanish for 'many'

non	French for 'no'
nous avons deux garçons ici	French for 'we have two boys here'
no way, José!	'that's never going to happen!'
oui	French for 'yes'
quelle horreur!	French for 'what horror!'
quelle surprise!	French for 'what a surprise!'
sacrebleu	French for 'gosh' or even 'blimey'
stupido	this is the Italian for 'stupid' – stupid!
-tastic	add this ending to any word to indicate a lot of something: e.g. 'Abs is braintastic'
très	French for 'very'
swoonsome	decidedly attractive
si, si, signor/signorina	Italian for 'yes, yes, mister/miss'
terriblement	French for 'terribly'
une grande	French for 'a big' – add the word 'genius' and you have the perfect description of Abs
Vogue	it's only the world's most influential fashion magazine, darling!
voilà	French for 'there it is'
what's the story, Rory?	'what's going on?'
what's the plan, Stan?	'which course of action do you think we should take?'
what the crusty old grandads?	'what on earth?'
zut alors!	French for 'darn it!'

Hi Megastar reader!

My name's Annabelle Starr*. I'm a fashion stylist – just like Soph's Aunt Penny – which means it's my job to help celebrities look their best at all times.

Over the years, I've worked with all sorts of big names, some of whom also have seriously big egos! Take the time I flew all the way to Japan to style a shoot for a girl band. One of the members refused to wear the designer number I'd picked out for her and insisted on sporting a dress her mum had run up from some revolting old curtains instead. The only way I could get her to take it off was to persuade her it didn't match her pet Pekingese's outfit!

Anyway, when I first started out, I never dreamt I'd write a series of books based around my crazy celebrity experiences, but that's just what I've done with Megastar Mysteries. Rosie, Soph and Abs have just the sort of adventures I wish my friends and I could have got up to when we were teenagers!

I really hope you enjoy reading the books as much as I enjoyed writing them!

Love **Annabelle**

* I'll let you in to a little secret: this isn't my real name, but in this business you can never be too careful!

Chapter One

The day before half-term is one of my favourites – it totally rocks! So far, all we'd done this time was mess around, and none of the teachers seemed to care. Even Mr Adams couldn't keep his mind on long division.

'So what's everyone getting up to during the holidays?' he asked, throwing aside a maths book and smiling at the class. 'Anything exciting?'

Abs let out a very un-Abs-like squeak, and me and Soph giggled. 'Exciting' didn't even come close to describing the fabuloso time we had planned!

I was just about to tell Mr Adams all about it, when Amanda Hawkins started flicking her hair around like she was in a shampoo advert. Amanda Hawkins has two hobbies – showing off and being mean. She always flicks her hair when she's about to say something smug. It's très annoying, let me tell you.

'I'm going to Jersey for the week,' Amanda boasted in a show-offy voice. 'My uncle has a hotel there. In fact, my uncle's hotel is actually the largest on the island. Five star, of course.'

'But of course!' I whispered under my breath.

Amanda turned around and glared at me. 'So what are you doing, Rosie Parker? Staying in boring Borehurst?'

'No, no. Me, Abs and Soph are going to stay at the Hotel Kesterton in London,' I said, sounding très sophisticated. 'James Piper's staying there while he rehearses for his new play, and the hotel manager has booked my mum's band to sing for him.'

A stunned silence fell over the class and Abs stifled a giggle.

So, OK, it totally sounded like one of my celeb-fuelled daydreams, but it really was true! My mum's Bananarama tribute band, the Banana Splits, had been chosen to play for James Piper. Oui, mes amis! *The* James Piper! The hugely talented, not to mention swoonsome, Hollywood actor! It was like I'd wandered into a parallel universe, where Mum's cringey music was actually cool. It was très weird.

Amanda's eyes slid from me, to Abs, to Soph and back to me again. Her mean little mind was obviously in overdrive.

'That's a lie, Rosie Parker!' she practically hissed. 'Why would your mum's tribute band be asked to play for James Piper? Get real.'

'I think you'll find that James is a big fan of eighties music and eighties tribute bands,' Soph explained.

Abs waved this week's copy of *Star Secrets* in the air, then started reading from an interview. '"James has always loved eighties music",' she read. '"It reminds him of his happy early teenage years with his younger brother, David, on their family's farm in Texas. The farm was so remote, the boys could only get two radio stations. One was country and western, which they both hated, and the other station played chart hits. James could listen all day long! He never got tired of that eighties vibe".'

'But I suppose if you're never going to meet him, you don't really need to know that,' Soph said in Amanda's direction.

'Well, that's very true, Soph,' I said, smiling kindly at Amanda, who had gone very red. 'Have you heard of the Hotel Kesterton, Amanda?'

'It's five star, of course,' Abs added with a glint in her eye.

* * *

It seemed about a million years until the next day. Nan came to wave us off at the train station, which was a good thing as we needed all the help we could get with Soph's massivo suitcase.

'I wanted to cover all fashion eventualities,' Soph explained. Not that she needed to explain herself to us. We're totally used to her fashionista ways.

'I find it's the shoes that make bags heavy,' Mum said helpfully.

Soph looked at her case thoughtfully. 'I only brought twelve pairs,' she said. 'Oh, and a couple of pairs of boots, and some sandals.'

Me and Abs started to giggle.

'If I didn't know you better, Sophie, I'd say you had a dead body in here!' Nan chuckled.

Honestly! Nan is always coming out with things like that. She watches waaay too many murder mysteries for her own good, if you ask me.

'I can't understand why you girls don't wear synthetic fabrics. They're easy to pack, light and funky,' Mum told Soph.

Hmmm. Sometimes it can be hard being the only one in the Parker household with a grip on reality. Nan thinks she's Jessica Fletcher from *Murder, She Wrote* and Mum reckons synthetic fabrics are cool. What chance do I have? I mean, I actually had to explain who James Piper was to Mum! Can you believe it? I just don't see how she could have missed all the stories about him in the paper. His brother's car accident last year was headline news, for, like, months. Zut alors, it was on the telly! The whole world held their breath while James sat by David's bedside in Los Angeles. It was très awful. At first, the doctors said that it was touch-and-go whether he'd make it, but little by little, David got better. That's how James met April, his gorgeous fiancée. She was one of his brother's nurses.

And just this week, the papers had been full of more stories about James. This time they were about his new play, *The Good Turn*, and his close friendship with British actress Polly McAllistair. Their fabuloso chemistry on stage had sparked pages and pages of gossip. All the papers were speculating about whether they were having an affair behind April's back. It was big news! But had Mum heard about any of it? Nah. Nope. Nada.

Luckily for Mum, I'd bought some press cuttings for her to read on the train. I might not have been able to drag her out of the eighties, but at least I could fill in a few of the missing years.

PIPER IS A SELL-OUT!

It's official, James Piper is set to star in the West End play, *A Good Turn*. But if you want to book tickets, you're already too late! They sold out as soon as the news was announced. We caught up with April, James's gorgeous fiancée, to find out more. 'Everyone with a ticket is in for a treat,' she told us. 'I've watched all the rehearsals and I have to say, this is the best role James has ever played.'

TWO OF A KIND

James Piper and British actress Polly McAllistair have been getting on like a house on fire during rehearsals for *A Good Turn*. According to our celebrity spy, the on-stage chemistry between James and Polly is sizzling hot. Could romance be on the horizon for these stage sweethearts? And what does April think of her fiancé's relationship with Polly? Watch this space, readers!

When our taxi drew up at the Hotel Kesterton, we were practically beside ourselves with excitement. The lobby was totally coolissimo! It was bigger than our school hall and pure white, with a très chic glass sculpture hanging from the ceiling.

Mum went to the reception desk to check us in while we perched on some white leather sofas and tried to look casual.

'Sacrebleu!' whispered Soph. 'It's James and April!'

'Where? Where?' Me and Abs jumped to our feet and looked around wildly. Sure enough, there were James and April, walking across the glittering lobby, right in front of us! April looked even more petite in real life. The light bounced off her glossy brown hair as she giggled at something James was saying.

A second later, Polly McAllistair stepped out of the lift. She looked just as gorgeous as April, though she was tall and blonde and had a totally different style. We held our breath, half-expecting there to be some kind of showdown, but April and Polly greeted each other with a kiss on both cheeks as if they were perfectly friendly. We shrugged at each other as they disappeared into the restaurant.

'Well,' Abs sighed, 'it just goes to show you can't believe everything you read in the papers.'

❋   ❋   ❋

We spent the next couple of hours unpacking and exploring the hotel. Me, Soph and Abs had a totally cool room. It was all pink and silver and there was even a seating area arranged around a chrome fireplace. Abs-the-cynic was convinced it was fake but Mum wouldn't let us light a fire to test it out. There was a solar-powered laptop and a huge-issimo telly too. Mum had the adjoining room with a connecting door so she could keep an eye on us.

Later, as we sat in the restaurant waiting for the Banana Splits to come on, I started feeling a bit wobbly. It was kind of hard to believe that James Piper was going to listen to Mum voluntarily. Don't get me wrong, I was totally proud of her . . . in theory . . . but the pride was kind of overshadowed by a severe attack of embarrassment. I mean, no girl wants to watch her mother strutting her 'funky stuff' – even if there are celebrities in the room. *Especially* if there are celebrities in the room! It was too much of a cringe-fest. As Mum's band took to the stage I couldn't bear to watch.

'Open your eyes, Rosie! James and April are totally loving it!' coaxed Abs. I hid behind my hands and groaned.

Abs nudged me in the ribs. 'Open. Your. Eyes.'

'No way, José!' I cried, squeezing my eyes even tighter.

'Go on,' soothed Abs. 'Everyone's enjoying it

. . . all the older ones, anyway.'

I didn't even want to imagine what was happening! Seriously!

'Is Mum making them dance? Argh! Don't tell me. I don't want to know.'

'Open your eyes, mon amie. Everyone's dancing,' Soph told me.

'No!' I said.

'Yes,' said Soph. 'It's really cool.'

'Au contraire, mon frère,' I said, shaking my head. 'Not possible.'

'Honestly, Rosie! It's totally not that bad!' Abs insisted.

'That's easy for you to say – she's not your mum!' I said, darkly.

Abs and Soph grabbed my hands and gently pulled them away from my face. I squinted through the smoke-machine clouds and saw James pulling April and Polly on to the dance floor. The whole restaurant was boogying to the Banana Splits. It was cringey. It was cool. It was weird.

After that, everything seemed to speed up.

Mum shimmied her way through Bananarama's greatest hits in what seemed like record time. Then suddenly she was sitting at our table sipping water and fanning herself with a dessert menu. I sat there, stunned, while people rushed up to congratulate her and the other members of the band. I was just thinking that life couldn't get any more surreal when Polly McAllistair came over and shook Mum's hand. Seriously! I am not joking!

'That was fabulous!' smiled Polly. 'I haven't danced that much in years!'

Within minutes, Mum and Polly were totally chatting like old friends.

'This is my daughter, Rosie, and these are her friends, Abs and Soph,' Mum said as we shook hands with Polly.

'You must be so proud of your mum,' smiled Polly.

'Er, yes. I'm glad you enjoyed the show,' I said, feeling dazed.

'I don't suppose you'd give us your autograph?' Mum asked.

Me, Abs and Soph grinned at each other – we'd all been dying to ask the same thing! Polly signed our restaurant menus while we told her how much we'd enjoyed her last film. Then she asked us all about ourselves and we chatted for ages.

'When James and April come back, I'll make sure you get their autographs too,' Polly told us. 'I think April wanted to call LA, so she's nipped upstairs to use the phone, and I don't know where James has got to – he's probably chatting with the play's director.'

We talked for a few more minutes, then Polly told us she had to go.

'She's so gorgeous close-up,' said Soph, as Polly disappeared into the crowd.

'She's a lovely person too,' I added. 'Totally down to earth.'

We talked about Polly for a while and then ordered some fizzy drinks. While we waited for them to come, we debated how well James Piper measured up to Maff, the gorgey singer from Fusion. As I pointed out, it was hard to compare them, because James was *much* more mature.

Suddenly, there was a commotion over by the door. The main lights whooshed on and we sat there, blinking in the glare.

'I apologise for the interruption to your evening,' the restaurant manager said into the stage microphone. 'I'm afraid there has been a burglary in the hotel. Expensive jewellery belonging to James Piper's fiancée has been stolen. I'd like to ask everybody to stay calm. The police are on their way and they'd like to interview everyone who is at the hotel this evening, so please remain in the restaurant.'

Me, Abs and Soph gawped at each other in shock. Sacrebleu! We were slap-bang in the middle of a celebrity mystery again!

Chapter Two

We watched, hawk-eyed, as the police set up a makeshift incident desk in the restaurant.

'Now then, ladies and gents,' said one of the detectives, 'my colleagues will be asking some of you to join us for an interview. Meanwhile, someone will be around to take your names and addresses.'

'Your nan will be very disappointed to have missed this,' said Abs, shaking her head regretfully.

Poor Nan. She'd stayed at home to watch the weeklong murder-mystery special on TV and now she was missing a real-life mystery!

'It is a shame,' I agreed.

Mum nodded. 'She'll be so cross when she finds out!'

I looked around the restaurant. Mum was right. Nan would be fuming. It was a complete and utter mystery-fest – there were police *everywhere*!

I winked at Abs and Soph. 'Luckily for April, there's a top team of celebrity sleuthers in the hotel, and I'm not talking about the police!' I whispered under my breath.

'Oui, oui, mon amie!' Abs whispered back.

'We are so going to bust this jewel thief!' hissed Soph a bit too loudly.

I glanced across at Mum. She hadn't heard a word. Très bon. Mum would totally not want us to get involved. Despite our fabuloso crime-busting track record, she didn't want me to get too close to any real crime – or real criminals for that matter. As far as she was concerned, danger, deception and crime were off the Parker menu. *Let the police deal with it, girls!* That's what she'd say.

Mum was taken off to be interviewed with the rest of the Banana Splits while we waited for someone to come over to our table and ask us questions.

'If we're going to help solve this crime, we need to find out exactly what's been stolen,' I said to the girls.

'And if there are any significant clues,' added Soph.

Abs gestured towards the incident desk, where the detectives were putting up huge-issimo screens. 'It doesn't look as if they're giving information away for free, amigos.'

'Well, we're not going to get very far without the facts,' I groaned.

'What we need is a cunning plan,' said Soph.

'I've got it!' yelled Abs with a grin. 'How about we interview the interviewer while they're interviewing us?'

'Like, what do you mean?' asked Soph, who was looking puzzled.

'Yeah, what's the plan, Stan?' I asked. That's the thing with having a friend whose brain is the size of a small planet. Sometimes Abs has to explain what she's thinking.

'The Dizzy Schoolgirl Routine,' Abs announced.

'The Dizzy Schoolgirl Routine?' gasped Soph.

'The Dizzy Schoolgirl Routine,' Abs repeated.

I sat back in my chair and thought for a bit. The Dizzy Schoolgirl Routine – the DSR for short – was based on Abs's brainless/harmless theory – i.e. if you act brainless, people will think you're harmless. It kind of makes sense. Seriously, if people think you're a total marshmallow brain, they're much more likely to let something slip. I mean, who's going to worry about what they say in front of a group of silly schoolgirls?

We all agreed it was worth a go.

'Here comes one of the hotel managers!' I hissed. 'Let's see if he'll tell us what we need to know!'

'Good evening, girls,' said the young man, pulling up a chair.

'Oooh, hello!' we giggled dizzily.

'The police have asked me to help out,' he said importantly. 'I just need to write down your details – names, ages, addresses, that kind of thing.'

'Are you a fan of James Piper?' Soph asked, gazing at the manager as if she hadn't heard a word he'd been saying.

'We think he's totally gorgey,' I cooed, waggling my head from side to side brainlessly. I learnt everything I know from Amanda Hawkins.

'He's yummy! Scrummy!' cried Abs, with a goofy grin.

'Ah, well, that's nice,' said the bemused hotel manager. 'Now, as I was saying, I just need your names and addresses for the police.'

He got out a notebook and Abs shot me a look. 'Do something,' she mouthed.

'Poor April,' I wailed quickly. 'Having her family jewels stolen like that!'

The manager looked at me blankly. 'Actually, it wasn't April's family jewels that were taken; it was her engagement ring and diamond necklace,' he said absent-mindedly

'Ooh,' cried Soph, clapping her hands to her mouth.

'Oh, now I'm not sure if I should have told you that,' said the young manager nervously.

'Told us what?' I giggled dizzily, taking the notebook and pen. 'Where shall I write my name?'

'Do you have a pink pen? I like pink pens best!' Soph beamed.

'What did you tell us?' cried Abs. 'Did I miss something? I hate missing things!'

'Never mind!' smiled the manager, looking relieved.

The DSR had worked like magic! I winked happily at the girls.

'Have any of you left the restaurant since the start of the show?' he asked.

We all shook our heads in unison.

Abs crossed her eyes slightly and grinned at the manager like a loon. 'I bet you know who did it! How clever! I wish I was as clever as you! Ooh, I like your tie!'

I stifled a laugh and stared at the table. Abs

was seriously hilarioso!

The young manager beamed proudly. 'Ah, I can't reveal our suspects, now can I?'

'You must have a few ideas,' Soph said, blinking innocently.

'None that I can tell you about,' replied the manager, straightening his back. 'And since you were all here when the robbery took place, there'll be no need for the police to interview you.' He scraped his chair back and stood up.

'Oh,' I said, feeling more than a little bit disappointed. After all, it would have been quite interesting to be interviewed by the police.

'So you know when the robbery took place . . .' Abs called, as the young man began to walk away.

He turned back to us and smiled. 'The jewels were there when April came down to dinner, but when she went up to make a phone call, they had gone. Now then, little ladies, isn't it past your bedtime?'

We nodded madly and waved at him as he set off across the restaurant.

'Toodle-oo!' called Abs, before we dissolved into fits of giggles.

* * *

Up in the room, we changed into our pyjamas and flopped onto the squashy sofas. The maid had lit candles in the fireplace and there was a très expensive-looking box of chocolates on the coffee table.

'Complimentary choccies! Yummissimo!' cried Abs, as she whipped off the lid.

'I could get used to this,' I grinned, stuffing a caramel into my mouth. Suddenly, I started cracking up again. 'Hey, Abs! Abs!'

'What?' said Abs, looking up from the chocolates.

'Toodle-oo,' I yelled, giving her a little wave.

'Toodle-oo, Abs!' giggled Soph, collapsing back into the cushions.

Abs chuckled as she munched her chocolate.

There was a knock on the adjoining door and

Mum came into the room. 'I'm off to bed, girls. Don't stay up too late.' She leant down and gave me a kiss on the cheek. 'Behave yourself, Rosie Parker! And you two,' she added, nodding towards Abs and Soph.

'Yeth, Mum!' I groaned through a mouthful of chocolate.

Once the door had clicked shut behind her, we started discussing the night's events.

'We've got heaps of info to go on after our award-winning performance!' I grinned.

'But not nearly enough to solve the crime,' Soph pointed out.

'I reckon it was an inside job,' Abs said. 'Think about it. The person who took April's jewellery must have known which room she and James were staying in.'

'But anyone could hang around and find out where they were staying,' I grabbed another chocolate and offered the box to Abs. 'Remember how we disguised ourselves as maids and snuck around the Hotel Londonia when we were helping the Sweetland sisters?' I passed the box over to Soph. 'What I mean is, anyone could have found out James and April's room number.'

'Hmmm,' said Abs. 'Maybe. But I still think it was an inside job.'

'There must be some clues somewhere,' Soph said thoughtfully. 'Thieves always leave something behind. Footprints, gloves, old photos . . .'

'Old photos?' I giggled. 'Have you been watching *Miss Marple* re-runs with Nan? No one would be daft enough to leave such an obvious clue.'

Soph shrugged. 'You may laugh, ma soeur, but there must be more evidence than we know about.'

I kicked thoughtfully against the sofa and stared at the flickering candles.

'We just need to think harder,' said Abs, breaking the silence. 'Maybe we could try the DSR on somebody else?'

'No,' I said. 'We don't want to arouse suspicion. I think we need to find those clues Soph was talking about.'

'But how are we going to do that?' Abs asked.

Me and Soph shrugged. We had no idea what to do next. But one thing was for sure – we were totally determined to solve the case and get April's diamonds back.

* * *

The next morning, we crept out of bed at the crack of dawn. Well, OK, it wasn't *exactly* the crack of dawn, but it was totally early for a weekend.

'So what's the story, Rory?' I asked.

'Let's just have a look around and see what we can see,' Soph suggested, as she lifted her foot off the floor and studied her shoe.

'Why don't we go down to the restaurant and see who's eating breakfast? It could be a très bon opportunity to ask the other guests a few questions,' I said.

'Coolissimo! But first I'm just going to change my shoes,' said Soph.

'Eh?' cried Abs. 'You've changed them about five times already and we haven't stepped outside the hotel room yet!'

'Yeah, but I'm not sure if it's a ballet-pump kind of day,' explained Soph.

Me and Abs looked down at our feet. We were both wearing ballet pumps.

'It totally *is* a ballet-pump kind of day,' Abs reassured her.

'Totally,' I nodded.

'But silver ones?' said Soph. 'Maybe I should wear the ones I customised with purple beads. And then maybe change my top to match.'

I looked at Abs and shrugged. We both knew where this was heading. There was no point in trying to hurry Soph when it came to fashion. She was totally unstoppable, like a tornado or a terrible disease. It was just best to let nature take its course.

'OK, Soph, but be quick, we don't want to miss any action,' I told her.

A quarter of an hour and two more shoe-changes later, we were just about to head out of the door when the posh hotel computer beeped.

We swivelled round in surprise.

'What's that?' I said.

Abs leaned over the keyboard and wiggled the mouse. 'It's an instant message from MurderMostHorrid – that's got to be your nan, Rosie!'

'No way! She's actually on IM now?' I gasped in surprise. 'You'd better get going without me. This might take a while . . .'

I sat down in front of the solar-powered laptop and read Nan's message:

MurderMostHorrid: Rosie, your mother's just been telling me about the robbery and I thought I'd get in touch right away. You know what she's like – she's more interested in the Banana Splits than something like this – but I knew that you'd have the facts. So, come on, tell me what's going on! I've just made a nice cuppa, and I've got plenty of time before *Diagnosis Murder* starts.

NosyParker: Hiya, Nan. I'm afraid we haven't got much to go on. So far we've found out that a diamond engagement ring and a diamond necklace were stolen.

MurderMostHorrid: Well, that's more than your mother knows! She told me it was 'jewellery'. 'What kind of jewellery?' I said. 'I don't know,' she said. 'Well,' I said, 'that's no help . . . '

NosyParker: Nan, I'm in kind of a hurry here!

MurderMostHorrid: Of course you are! You've got plenty of detecting to do. Try and put yourself in Miss Marple's frame of mind, Rosie. Now, she's very good at solving crimes in hotels . . .

NosyParker: Right. Bye, then!

MurderMostHorrid: Wait – I want you to promise that you'll let me know as soon as anything happens. Call me any time, day or night! I'm here to help!

NosyParker: Er, thanks, Nan. That's good to know. I'll be in touch soon.

MurderMostHorrid: Cheerio for now, then! And remember, if you get stuck, just ask yourself what Miss Marple would do.

NosyParker: Er, whatever, Nan. Got to go! x

MurderMostHorrid: Good luck, Rosie! x

I turned the laptop off and quickly slipped out of the door. Poor Nan, she was seriously fed up that she was missing all the action!

As I made my way down the hallway, I thought about what Abs had said. Was it really an inside job? I was so deep in thought, I almost walked straight past one of the police detectives I'd seen the previous day.

I quickly ducked behind a huge pot plant and pretended to tie my shoelace. OK, so technically my ballet pumps didn't *have* laces, but I was hoping the detective wouldn't pay as much attention to shoes as Soph always does.

Just then, the detective's phone started to ring. I seriously couldn't believe my luck – prime eavesdropping potential!

'Hello, guv. We checked the CCTV but it's been disabled, so we don't have pictures of the thief,' said the detective. 'We sent a couple of samples off to forensics: a long hair – probably a woman's – and a bluish creamy substance that we found smeared on the door of April's room and the drawer where the jewellery was kept. I can't for the life of me work out what it is, boss, but we only found it in those two places. Nowhere else. Should get the results pretty quick. I'll let you know what they say.'

I watched the detective put his phone in his pocket and stride off down the hall.

At last! A clue! Two clues, to be exact. Let's face it, I hadn't lost my touch in the earwigging department! Nan would be totally proud. I made up my mind to IM her later and rushed downstairs to tell the girls what I'd heard.

Chapter Three

'I knew it!' squealed Abs. 'It was an inside job. The blue stuff was only on the door and the drawer – that totally proves that the thief didn't have to search around. He or she knew exactly where to find the jewels.'

'Eh?' said Soph, looking blank.

'Don't you see? If they'd been looking around for the diamonds, the blue stuff would have been all over the room!' Abs explained.

'Oh yeah,' said Soph.

I crunched a spoonful of cornflakes thoughtfully. Surely there was something else the clues could tell us? I wished the detective had mentioned what colour the hair was. That would have shortened the list of suspects a bit.

'Look, it's James!' said Abs, nudging me and Soph.

'Ooh, he's such a beau garçon!' sighed Soph.

We watched James walk over to the table where Polly was sitting. She jumped up with a huge grin and gave him a massivo hug.

Suddenly a figure in the doorway caught my eye. It was April. But something was wrong. Her lips were pressed together in an angry line. She looked totally different. It was weirdissimo. But then, I could imagine what it must have been like for her. I mean, she'd just had her precious jewellery stolen – no wonder she was annoyed. And it couldn't have been easy coping with all the rumours about James and Polly, day after day. The pressure was probably getting to her.

I turned back to the girls. 'Mum wanted to know if you fancied going on the London Eye today, with her and the band,' I said.

'Bien sûr, ma soeur!' cried Abs.

'Coolissimo!' Soph squealed.

At that very second, I spotted the detective I'd overheard on the phone. He was striding across the restaurant, flanked by two uniformed officers. We stared in disbelief as they marched purposefully over to the table where James and Polly were sitting.

'What the crusty old grandads is going on?!' I cried, as the detective clamped his hand on Polly's shoulder.

Polly turned towards him, her smile fading. Then he pulled her briskly to her feet and got out a pair of handcuffs.

QUELLE HORREUR! HE WAS GOING TO ARREST POLLY FOR STEALING APRIL'S JEWELLERY!

We watched in utter shock as the police read Polly her rights. Then for a second everything froze, as if we were in a movie and someone had pressed 'pause'. Nobody moved. Nobody spoke.

It was très tense, let me tell you.

Suddenly, there was a horrible 'click' as the handcuffs snapped around Polly's wrists.

'But I haven't done anything!' she protested to the silent room.

The detectives were trying to lead her away, but she was frozen to the spot. 'James! April! I didn't do it. Please believe me. I DIDN'T DO IT!'

We could see Polly's shoulders shaking from where we were sitting. She was taking huge, heaving breaths. She looked totally petrified.

James jumped to his feet and reached out towards her. 'Polly, it's OK. It's OK. We believe you,' he said soothingly.

Polly let out an enormous sob and James turned to the police. 'There has clearly been a huge mistake. Polly is our friend. She'd never do anything to hurt us.'

The police shook their heads at James, and April laid a restraining hand on his arm. I could see her lips moving from across the room but I could only make out a few words. I'm almost sure she was telling him to let the police do their job, but it was hard to say for certain.

James sat down slowly as Polly was marched away. His gorgeous eyes were filled with concern and shock. You could so tell he was totally devastated. April leaned in behind James and wrapped her arms around him. She rested her chin on his shoulder and watched Polly as she left the room.

There was a moment of stunned silence, then everyone turned back to their tables and went on eating their breakfast.

I let out a long, gasping breath. I couldn't believe it. Polly McAllistair, British actress extraordinaire, a thief?

Me, Abs and Soph were still staring at each other in horror when Mum rushed into the restaurant. She'd just seen Polly being led through the lobby in handcuffs.

'What on earth are the police doing with that lovely Polly McAllistair?' she asked.

We quickly explained what had happened, but

as we went over the dramatic events, I couldn't help feeling that something didn't quite add up. It was so clear that James and Polly had a bond, so why on earth would Polly steal his fiancée's jewellery? It just didn't make sense.

* * *

A few hours later, we were dangling at least a million metres above the ground, in a capsule on the London Eye. It was totally coolissimo – looking down on the River Thames and Big Ben – but we couldn't really keep our minds on sightseeing. We had more important matters to discuss.

'I can't help thinking that things aren't as simple they seem,' I said. 'Why would Polly want to steal anything anyway? I mean, she's an international actress. She's fabulously rich. She's worth millions!'

Soph looked at me seriously. 'But sometimes that doesn't make any difference. You've read the stories about the celebs who go loop-tastic and steal stuff from shops.'

'Si si, signorina, it's not always about the money.'
Abs said wisely. 'Sometimes it's psychological.'

I still wasn't convinced. Polly had been so
balanced and happy when we'd talked to her the
previous night. She definitely hadn't seemed like a
celeb in meltdown, teetering on the brink of a
thieving frenzy!

'And what about April?' Abs said. 'If she'd
believed Polly was innocent, she would have tried
to stop the arrest.'

We looked down at the teeny people scurrying
around on the ground. I was thinking so hard it
felt like my head was going to explode!

'I dunno,' I said. 'This whole thing is fishier
than a supermarket fish counter. I mean, why
would Polly steal April's stuff? We spoke to her just
yesterday and she didn't seem to be behaving
weirdly. We've met enough celebs to be able to
read the signs, and she didn't seem like someone in
trouble – did she?'

'Hmm,' said Abs, leaning up against the glass.

'You're probably right.'

'But that doesn't explain why April didn't stop the arrest. Like Abs says, she would have stepped in if she thought Polly was innocent.'

The wheel turned, lifting us higher in the sky as our top sleuthing brains turned over the evidence. I could see the tip of Soph's tongue poking out of the side of her mouth, like it does when she's solving maths problems. Seriously, if the London Eye could have used our brainpower as electricity, it would have been whizzing around at about a hundred miles an hour!

'I just wish we knew what April said to James when they were handcuffing Polly,' I said. 'That might give us an idea. I think it must have been, "Let the police do their job," but I'm just not sure. I couldn't quite make out the words.'

'They should totally put lip-reading on the school curriculum!' sighed Soph.

'Bien sûr, ma soeur,' I nodded.

'Maybe we can work it out by process of elimination,' Abs suggested. 'Could she have been saying something else, like . . .'

'Like what?' I wailed in frustration. '"I like corn on the cob"? "Is that man's first name Bob?"? How are we ever going to know for sure?'

'Well, even if we can't work out what she said, we still saw what she did,' Soph pointed out.

'More like what she didn't do,' I said darkly. 'I reckon Polly must have done something to make April wary of her. I don't mean all that silly newspaper stuff – something else, something that would make April stop James from getting rid of the police.'

'You're right,' Abs nodded. 'April was definitely trying to stop James.'

'Which means she's one hundred per cent certain that Polly did it,' said Soph.

I looked across at the London skyline. 'I hope she's wrong.'

Just then, Mum came to stand beside me. I didn't need to worry about her earwigging on our conversation – she'd been deep in discussion with the band. She peered down and gripped her guidebook until her knuckles turned white. Poor Mum. She hates heights!

'Rosie . . .' she said weakly.

'Hmmm?' I replied.

'Do you think Soph would be interested in helping us with our stage costumes? We haven't quite worked out what we're going to wear at tonight's gig.'

Mum has an embarrassing habit of calling her Banana Splits performances 'gigs'. But what can you do?

I glanced across at Soph, who was fiddling with her skirt and staring intently at her reflection in the glass. She pursed her lips like a model and struck a pose. Even the whole of London couldn't compete with Soph's love of fashion.

'Do Girls Aloud wear short skirts?' I said.

'Eh?' said Mum.

'Never mind,' I groaned. 'Let me go and ask her for you.'

* * *

When we arrived back at the hotel that afternoon, we headed to the shiny marble reception desk to pick up our room keys.

'I understand you have another guest in your party, Mrs Parker,' said the pretty receptionist.

Mum looked bewildered. 'No, there's just the four of us,' she said, gesturing to me and the girls.

'She means the five of us,' said a familiar voice. WHAT THE CRUSTY OLD GRANDADS? I spun round and there was Nan, looking all smart in a beige skirt and an anoraky-blazer type of thing.

I sighed heavily. All the telltale signs were there – the sensible shoes, the set perm, the nosey expression – NAN HAD DRESSED UP AS JESSICA FLETCHER AGAIN! And when Nan got kitted out like her favourite *Murder, She Wrote* star, it could mean only one thing . . .

'I've come to help you solve the crime!' she hissed happily in my ear.

Fabulous. Great. Marvelloso.

'Well, what a lovely surprise!' said Mum, totally

oblivious to what Nan had just said. 'Let's all go and have some afternoon tea. You must be feeling a bit peckish after the train-ride up.'

We walked over to the corner of the lobby where a group of dazzlingly white chairs were arranged around a glass table. Just as we were sitting down, one of the hotel managers came over.

'Mrs Parker? Can I have a word in private?'

'Yes, of course,' said Mum, getting back up and following her across the lobby.

Nan watched them leave and beamed around the table at us. 'After you told me about the robbery, I couldn't stay at home! A real-life robbery is much better than watching Murder-Mystery Week on the telly!' She settled comfortably into her chair. 'Now girls, I don't want you to worry any more! I'm here now and I'm going to help you solve this dreadful crime.'

Me, Abs and Soph are totally capable of solving mysteries on our own, thanks, I thought. I hadn't the heart to say it out loud, though.

We ordered a pile of cakes and waited for Mum to get back. After fifteen minutes, she hurried across the lobby and sank into her chair. 'OK, listen up, girls,' she said, a serious look on her face. 'I've just been speaking to the hotel manager and she wants everything to go on as normal. The Banana Splits are still going to sing tonight. She wants it to be as if nothing bad has happened. Under no circumstances are you to go bothering James and April. That means no creeping around and no asking questions. Got it, Rosie?'

I nodded. 'Got it.'

'Got it, Soph? Got it, Abs?' said Mum.

'Got it, Mrs P,' said the girls.

Suddenly, Mum looked at her watch and jumped about three metres in the air. 'Look at the time! I've got to get to band rehearsals!' she shrieked and looked sadly at the pile of chocolate éclairs. She hadn't even had time to eat one. 'See you later, girls! Oh, and thanks for all your fashion tips earlier!'

'No worries!' said Soph. 'Can't wait to see you on stage!'

We watched her darting across the lobby, this time in the direction of the restaurant.

'Right,' said Nan. 'Well, your mother didn't say anything about *me* investigating the mystery, did she? So tell me everything that's happened and don't miss anything out. All the details count in a case like this.'

I rolled my eyes – as if we didn't know that already! We began explaining all about the robbery and the arrest, munching our way through the pile of cakes as we talked. We each took it in turns to tell our own version of the events. Nan nodded along as we spoke but refused to eat the cakes – she'd brought a packet of custard creams along in her handbag. She whipped them out and dipped them in her tea, ignoring the astonished face of the waitress. I was mortified. On the other hand, it meant more cakes for us. Yippee!

'So,' I said, after we'd finished the story, 'have you come up with a cunning plan?'

Nan shook her head. 'Not to worry, though. I'll think of something.'

Just at that very second, who should walk through the door but Polly McAllistair! SERIOUSLY!!! She was with a smart man who was holding a briefcase. We leaned over towards the reception desk to earwig on their convo.

'Good afternoon. I am Miss McAllistair's lawyer,' said the briefcase man. 'Polly has been let out on bail and she is to stay at the hotel and continue with rehearsals for her play. But I need your guarantee that you will keep the press away. No photos. No interviews. No questions. Keep the guests away from her. Miss McAllistair is not to be bothered.'

The hotel manager nodded and shook Polly's hand, welcoming her back. Then Polly and her lawyer headed towards the lift.

Nan nodded wisely at us and smiled as if she'd suddenly worked something out. 'Now I have a plan!' she said, and jumped up from her chair.

'What, Nan? What?' I hissed.

She tapped her index finger on the side of her nose and hurried off towards the lift.

'Stop!' squeaked Abs in alarm.

'Come back!' I gasped, but it was too late. Nan was already getting into the lift with Polly and her lawyer.

We stared in horror. What the flaming trousers was she up to now?

Chapter Four

Ten hideous outfits Mum has worn on stage:

1. Dungarees, army boots and pink fingerless gloves – hmmm
2. Electric-blue hot pants. Somebody call the fashion police!
3. A lemon-yellow ra-ra-skirt-dress-thing with white stilettos (I'm not joking)
4. A shiny gold leotardy top – yup
5. A pink flamenco dress with matching hair-band-scarf-thing

6. Zut alors!
7. This is waaay too traumatic!
8. I can't go on!!!
9. I just can't!!!
10. Let's just say that the Banana Splits is a style-free zone – I think you get the picture

We were back in the restaurant, watching my mum strut her stuff with the Banana Splits. Soph was grinning from ear to ear. I couldn't believe that she was actually responsible for choosing the band's outfits. I mean, Soph is always giving us fashion advice and OK, you could call some of her fashion choices a bit on the bold side, but usually you can count on her to come up with the goods. So when Mum put her in charge of styling the group for that night's show, I thought Soph might tone their look down a bit, what with her being a *Vogue*-reading fashion-bunny.

Oh, how wrong I was!

Mum was grooving away in front of the entire restaurant, wearing a tight pair of fake snakeskin trousers (chosen by Soph) teamed with a leather waistcoat (chosen by Soph). Oh, and she had backcombed hair, too (Soph again). Not a look that any mother should be sporting, I think you'll agree. Sometimes I seriously worry about Soph's sanity.

'It's totally fashion-forward,' Soph explained. 'Backcombed hair and all that late eighties rock-chick stuff is coming back in style.'

I gave her an unconvinced look.

'No, don't be like that, Rosie. Fashion goes in cycles. You'll all be wearing this kind of thing soon,' Soph enthused. 'It's all in this month's issue of *Vogue!*'

I stared at the front of the restaurant, where Mum was wiggling her snakeskinned bum to the beat. *Fashion-forward? Those trousers? Like, hel-lo, Soph? I think not.*

'Somebody. Get. Me. A. Blindfold,' I said through gritted teeth.

My brilliant mystery radar was being totally compromised. How could I think clearly with Nan missing in action (doing who knows what) and Mum dressed like an escapee from a Halloween party?

It was totally weird though, because despite the cringeworthy outfits, the audience were l-o-v-i-n-g the band's performance. The heavy atmosphere that had been hanging over the hotel since the robbery had dissolved like a tooth in a glass of cola. I couldn't deny it. My mum was a big hit amongst the fabulously rich and famous.

A few minutes into the show, Nan bustled up to our table. She looked massively pleased with herself.

'What happened?' I whispered to her urgently. 'Did you find anything out?'

'Let me have a second to collect my thoughts,' she said with a simper, picking up the dinner menu and looking up and down the list. 'Would you look at these prices, Rosie? I ask you! Fancy paying all that money for fish and chips!'

I opened my mouth to tell her that all our meals were totally free because of Mum performing at the hotel. But it was too late. Nan was already off on one.

'Look at what the waiter is carrying over there!' she said, energetically. 'That little lot will have cost a fortune! Somebody will be paying a pretty penny tonight!'

With perfect timing, the waiter started walking towards our table. Nan eyed the three plates he was balancing along his arm. She couldn't believe it when he handed a massivo helping of pasta to Abs, a huge prawn salad to Soph and a great big plate of fish and chips to me.

'Rosie!' she hissed. 'That will cost your mother a fortune!'

'It's all right Nan. It's fr–' I started.

'It is not all right, Rosie Parker!' Nan interrupted. 'You should have brought yourself a nice packed supper instead of this nonsense! That serving of fish and chips cost eight times more than it would at Trotters!'

Trotters was Nan's fave Borehurst hang-out. She spent more time there than she did at home.

And OK, it was totally true. The fish and chips at the Kesterton did cost loads more – but as they were on the house, it really didn't matter!

'Would Madame like to order from the dinner menu?' the waiter asked Nan politely.

Nan looked at him in utter horror. Honestly, you'd think he'd just asked her to go skinny-dipping in the Thames or something. It was hilarioso. 'Certainly not, young man!' she cried indignantly. 'I wouldn't dream of it!'

I started frantically trying to get her attention to tell her that dinner was free, but she looked at me like I was about five and told me to stop fidgeting.

'Come on, Nana Parker, you must want something,' Soph said encouragingly.

'I ate a big lunch on the train!' Nan said firmly. All the same, she eyed our steaming plates enviously. (Well, technically Soph's salad wasn't steaming, but you know what I mean.)

'Hmmm, maybe I'll have a cup of tea and a toasted teacake. But make it the cheapest one on the menu!' she told the waiter.

I sighed heavily. Who cared about the cost of stupido teacakes? I was more interested in what Nan had found out about Polly!

'Nevermindaboutthemoneyit'sallfreecosofmum,' I said at top speed, before Nan could start complaining again. 'OK, so, what's the story, Rory? Er, I mean, tell us what happened with Polly!'

'FREE!' Nan cried. 'Well, why didn't you say so, Rosie?'

AAARRRRRRRRRGGGGGGGGGGHHHH HHHHHH!!!

Abs and Soph disappeared behind a dessert menu. I could see the tops of their heads shaking with laughter as Nan called the waiter back and ordered a large portion of fish and chips.

'Nan, tell us what happened with Polly,' I demanded, nearly jumping up and down with frustration.

'Let's just wait for my dinner to get here,' Nan suggested.

'Argh!!!' I cried. 'Please tell us what happened!'

'Honestly, Rosie, you have no patience at all!' said Nan, as Soph and Abs hiccupped and snorted behind the menu. 'Well, when Polly and her lawyer got into the lift, I followed them up to the fourth floor. Nobody suspects an old lady of being up to anything! Look at Miss Marple and Jessica Fletcher – they could get away with murder if they wanted to.'

'I thought the whole point was for Miss Marple and Jessica Fletcher to solve the crimes rather than commit them,' said Abs, coming out from behind the menu.

I gave Abs the death stare. She so didn't realise how easy it was to distract Nan. At this rate, we'd never hear what had happened.

'Well, yes, that's right, dear . . .' Nan started.

'Go *on*, Nan,' I said firmly, kicking Abs under the table.

'Oh – yes. Now, where was I? Well, I followed them until they got to the room, then I waited until Polly's lawyer had left and went to knock on her door.'

'YOU DID *WHAT*?' I spluttered, practically choking on a chip.

'I knocked on her door,' Nan repeated. 'At first she didn't want to chat, but I mentioned you three girls and your mother's band and she soon invited me in!'

Me, Soph and Abs grinned at each other.

'I don't like to beat about the bush, as you know, girls,' said Nan. 'So I asked straight out if she'd had anything to do with the robbery.'

Soph dropped the fork she was holding and stared at Nan.

'Well, poor Polly burst into tears and told me that she was completely innocent, but it was her hair that the police had found in the room. Of course, everyone knew that the hair could have got there any time, since Polly often visited April and James in their suite – she even borrowed April's hairbrush the other day.' Nan paused dramatically to see if we had all realised the significance of that and we nodded at her to go on. 'So of course the police couldn't use her hair as evidence. But apparently it was the smudges of blue cream that caused all the problems. Polly uses an expensive moisturiser called –'

'*Midnight Dew!*' I finished. I'd read all about Polly's beauty regime in *Star Secrets*.

'That's right, dear,' nodded Nan. 'She told me that when she was the face of that fancy cosmetics company, Jacques Mystic, they gave her a lifetime's supply. But the cream was discontinued two years ago, which means – '

'Hardly anybody else still uses it!' finished Abs.

'Clever girl, Abigail! Nobody uses it but Polly, so the police assumed that she must be the thief. But Polly is convinced that somebody used the face cream to frame her!' Nan folded her hands in front of her and looked at us one by one. 'Well, after we'd had a little chat about that, I remembered you girls talking about all the rumours in the papers. So I asked Polly if there was anything going on between her and that James Hyper.'

'YOU *WHAT*?' Soph shrieked.

'I'm not one to mince my words, Sophie McCoy!' Nan said proudly. 'Well, at first she told me that she and James were just friends, but when I pressed her, she admitted that she did have feelings for him!'

'She would never do anything to split up James and April, though,' I said.

'That's what she told me,' Nan replied. 'She told me that she thinks the world of April. She would never do anything to hurt them. That's why she has kept her feelings hidden.'

'Zut alors, Nana Parker! Not even a professional journalist could have wormed out a secret like that,' cried Soph, looking totally impressed.

'Polly's secret is safe with me,' smiled Nan. 'I'm not likely to go running to the papers.'

'Go on with the story, Nan. Did you come down to the restaurant straight away?'

'What did you do after Polly confided in you?' asked Abs at the same time.

Nan leaned forward. 'I gave her a big hug and

promised her that we'd solve the crime between us and clear her name for good.'

'And we totally will,' I cried. I just didn't exactly know how.

'Here!' said Abs, throwing me a paper napkin. 'Let's make a list of things we already know. It might help us think.'

Things we already know:

1. Polly has been framed
2. Only five people believe she is innocent: me, Soph, Abs, Nan and James Piper
3. The person who framed her knew her beauty regime

'Everyone knew her beauty regime; it was in *Star Secrets*,' Soph pointed out.

I crossed out number three on the napkin, and wrote this instead:

3. Polly has secret feelings for James

'You'd better not write that down, Rosie – somebody might see it,' said Abs.

I groaned and torn the napkin into tiny shreds. 'How on earth are we going to prove that Polly is innocent?' I wailed helplessly.

'Je ne sais pas!' replied Soph.

We stared at our empty plates in silence. We seriously did not have a clue.

Chapter Five

I had been so gripped by Nan's story, I hadn't even noticed Mum had stopped singing. She came over to our table, beaming happily.

'That was our best performance yet! Don't you think, girls?'

There was a pause, then everyone – including Nan – started nodding enthusiastically, even though we'd missed most of it.

'Ooh, yes!' fibbed Nan.

'Marvelloso,' I told her, crossing my fingers.

'Lovin' the shimmying, Mrs P!' Soph added

with a convincing grin.

I suddenly felt a bit guilty that we hadn't watched the show, but then Mum's snakeskin trousers started squeaking against her chair and my guilt turned into embarrassment. Why can't Mum wear silent trousers like other mothers? This was SERIOUSLY CRINGEVILLE!

Suddenly, everyone fell silent. I looked up and there was Polly McAllistair, right in the middle of the restaurant! She was wearing a très chic emerald-green dress that floated behind her as she walked between the tables. She so didn't look like a shifty diamond thief.

Polly walked up to James and April's table and gave them a smile.

'Sorry, darling,' April said coldly, in a voice that carried around the room. 'All these seats are taken.'

We watched in horror as Polly looked at the empty seats around the table.

'No, April's getting mixed up,' smiled James. 'Nobody's joining us for dinner. Sit down, Polly.'

April turned to James. 'I think you're forgetting that the Carters are dining with us this evening.' Her voice was light but she was trying too hard. April was lying. I was certain of it.

Polly took a few steps backwards, her face crumpling with distress. I tried to give her an encouraging smile and Nan pulled out a chair, but Polly didn't notice. She was way too upset.

Just then, one of the waiters approached Polly. 'Where will you be sitting this evening, Madame?'

I tried to catch her eye again to beckon her over, but she still didn't see me.

'Where will you be sitting, Madame?' repeated the waiter.

Polly faltered. 'I've . . . I've changed my mind,' she said, turning to rush out of the restaurant.

We watched the emerald silk of her dress disappear out of the door.

James leapt to his feet but April hissed at him to sit down.

'But I can't remember inviting the Carters! The seats are free!' cried James.

'The Carters aren't coming!' April snapped. 'It was just an excuse. I do not want to spend the evening with the woman who has been arrested for stealing my jewellery.' Suddenly, her voice softened and she looked at James adoringly. 'It will be nice to spend some time alone too.'

James glanced at the door, and slumped back in his seat. I could totally tell he was thinking about Polly.

✳ ✳ ✳

We decided to go for a late stroll around the block to see if some fresh air would help us come up with a cunning plan.

'I've got to go to a band meeting, so I'll pop into your room later to say goodnight,' Mum told us. She walked off towards the lift, her trousers squeaking as she went. 'Don't go too far from the hotel and keep out of trouble!' she called over her shoulder.

'And you keep away from snakes,' I called back. 'They might want to make friends with your trousers.'

Abs began to giggle quietly and Mum gave me a withering look.

'What can I say, Mrs P? Rosie just doesn't get fashion,' Soph called to Mum.

'Oi! Do you mind?' I cried.

Soph flashed me and Abs a smile. 'You'll both be wearing the same thing in a few months' time. Just you wait!'

I shuddered. Soph's fashion predictions had a strange tendency to come true. Let's just hope she was wrong about this one. I mean, a world full of people wearing snakeskin trousers? How creepy would that be?!

'Well,' said Nan, cutting through my thoughts, 'I'm off to catch the end of *Midsomer Murders*. A spot of telly might help me think of something to help poor Polly. Cheerio!'

As I watched Nan walking towards the lift, a disturbing image of her dressed in snakeskin trousers popped into my mind. AAARGGHHH! I shook my head wildly – the mere thought of Nan in anything made out of snakeskin made me cringe all the way down to my toes.

We set off across the lobby again. We were just at the door when we caught sight of James and April. They were standing by the marble reception desk, and judging by the way April was stamping her feet, they were in the middle of a très heated discussion!

I winked at the girls and we changed direction, walking over to a nearby tourist-information stand. Soph picked up a *What's On in London* leaflet and we stared at it intently while we strained to listen.

'I can't stand it, James. I just can't!' April was saying. 'I want my engagement ring back, and my necklace. They mean so much to me!'

I peered through a gap in the stacks of leaflets on the stand and saw James put his arm around April. 'I know, honey, but the police are investigating the wrong person,' he said soothingly.

'How can you be so sure?' April asked.

'I've known Polly for years. She's not a thief!' James said gently.

'Then tell me why she was arrested! Tell me where my diamonds are. Tell, me, James! Tell me!' April began sobbing. It was mucho dramatico.

Soph raised her eyebrows at me and we turned back to squint through the gap.

'I don't know what happened. If I did, Polly wouldn't be in this mess!' cried James, his eyes looking troubled.

'That girl stole my jewellery and you're on her side!' screamed April.

James pulled his arm away and looked his fiancée in the eye. 'Polly is innocent, April. I believe it from the bottom of my heart. She had nothing to do with the robbery.'

'She's been arrested for it!' April hissed. 'The police have no doubt, and neither do I! She's guilty and I don't want her anywhere near us! I want her to leave the hotel and I want you to talk to the director of the play. I want her fired! I won't have you working with her. Not after what she's done!'

Abs let out a gasp and I nudged her in the ribs.

'Calm down, honey,' begged James. 'I know you're upset about the diamonds, but you've got to see sense. Polly isn't a thief. She's a friend. There's been a huge misunderstanding. I'm standing by her, and so is the director. The play wouldn't be the same without her. She's innocent. You've got to see that!'

'I haven't got to see anything!' April screamed. She stormed off on her high heels, barging into the stand where we were hiding.

James stared after April as she stomped out of the hotel. He looked totally distraught. He ran his hand through his hair and sighed helplessly.

We didn't want him to notice that we'd been eavesdropping, so we took some leaflets and strolled casually out of the door, talking loudly about sightseeing as we went.

The sound of the London traffic roared in my ears as we stood on the pavement outside.

'Zut alors!' I gasped. 'Talk about complicated! April is convinced that Polly did it, but James is convinced she didn't! We know Polly's innocent, but why is April so certain she's not? Did you hear what she said in there?'

Abs nodded. 'Oui.'

'She was pretty full-on,' Soph added.

'How the dancing monkeys are we going to get to the bottom of this mystery?' I cried.

'Beats me,' replied Soph.

'I don't know what's wrong with us,' said Abs. 'We've solved trickier mysteries than this before now, but this diamond robbery has got us stumped. We must be losing our celeb-sleuthing powers!'

'Au contraire, mon frère!' I said, pointing as I spotted April's figure at the bottom of the road. 'Come on!'

We could see April rummaging furiously in her bag as we belted down the street. She raised her arm to flag down a cab, then hitched her bag on to her hip and carried on rummaging.

'That girl is desperate to find something,' Abs puffed.

'Maybe she's looking for lipgloss,' Soph panted.

'Or tissues,' I said, looking at the angry tears tracking down April's cheeks.

April dropped the bag on the ground and crouched down. She began searching through all her stuff. She pulled out a purse, followed by a notebook and a hairbrush, then she muttered angrily and shoved them all back in again.

'Sacrebleu! She has seriously lost it. Maybe we should do something?' I said.

Just then, the shiny black cab she had hailed screeched up to the kerb, having done a U-turn. April jumped up and yanked the door open.

'She is in a très grande hurry!' breathed Abs.

As April flung her bag into the cab, I saw something drop out of it and land in the gutter. Without thinking, I began running towards the cab. 'Hey, April, wait!' I yelled, as I pounded up to the door.

April scrambled on to the back seat and turned to me. 'I'm not in the mood for James's little fans. Leave me alone!' She slammed the door in my face and shouted something to the cab driver.

I stared at her through the window with my mouth open in shock. 'But something fell out of your handbag!' I murmured pointlessly, as the cab roared off down the road.

I crouched down to see what April had dropped. Maybe I was wrong. But it really had seemed as if something had fallen out of her bag. Something small. Something shiny. Something like . . . zut alors! I dropped to my knees by the side of the road.

Abs and Soph raced over, just as I found something small and circular hidden in all the rubbish in the gutter. My hands were grey with dirt but something was sparkling between my fingers. It was a diamond ring, threaded on to a matching diamond necklace.

'I don't believe it, Rosie!' gasped Abs. 'It's the missing jewellery!'

Chapter Six

We crouched by the side of the road and gawped at the dusty diamonds.

'Forget going for a walk, this calls for an emergency meeting,' I said, tucking the jewellery into the pocket of my jeans.

We dashed back to the hotel and skidded across the marble floor of the lobby. When we got into the lift, I jabbed hard at the 'up' button.

I put my hand in my pocket and touched the diamonds. Polly was going to be so thrilled when we told her that we'd found them!

'Is it me or is this lift going slower than normal?' said Abs.

Soph tapped her foot impatiently.

I looked at the numbers above the door. We had been on '3' for a long time. What if the lift was stuck and we couldn't get out? What if we were actually trapped? How would we help Polly then? The hotel would have to call the fire brigade or something. Or one of the other guests would have to save us. Someone fit and strong and brave and gorgey, like James Piper! I stared into space, imaging James climbing down to rescue us. Ooh, la la! Now that would be cool!

Suddenly, Abs pulled at my arm. 'Earth calling Rosie. Er, hello? Diamonds? Mystery? Emergency meeting?'

I snapped back into mystery-solving mode as the lift doors pinged open. A few seconds later we were pelting down the hallway to Nan's room.

'Open up, Nan!' I yelled, hammering hard on her door.

'Let us in, Nana Parker!' cried Soph.

The door opened a few centimetres and Nan peered out. She was clearly not happy to see us. 'I've just sat down to watch the second part of *Midsomer Murders*,' she grumbled.

'Never mind about that! Look at this!' I pulled the ring and necklace out of my pocket and held it for Nan to see. It swung backwards and forwards between my fingers.

'Well, blow me down!' said Nan, throwing the door open. 'Don't stand outside dithering, come in!' We piled into the room and Nan kicked the door shut with her fluffy slipper. 'Pass me my reading glasses, Rosie. I need to see this close up.'

* * *

Half an hour later, we'd explained everything to Nan and were sleuthing for all we were worth.

'We need to think of some answers,' I said. 'Like how did April end up with her own stolen diamonds?'

'Maybe they were never stolen in the first

place,' said Soph thoughtfully. 'Maybe April put them in her bag and forgot they were there.'

'But that doesn't explain how Polly's moisturiser got all over April's room,' Abs pointed out. 'It was smeared over the door handle and the drawer where April kept her jewellery – who put it there?'

Nan crunched into a bourbon biscuit as I paced up and down the room. It was obvious that the jewellery meant the world to April, and when you care about something that much, you don't just forget where you've put it, do you? I mean, I'm always losing my maths book, because, let's face it, maths sucks. But give me a bar of chocolate and it's an entirely different matter. Seriously, it would be completely impossible for me to forget where I'd put my chocolate. The same thing must go for really expensive, sentimentally important jewellery. April would just never forget where she put her diamonds.

Suddenly I stopped pacing and looked at the girls and Nan, totally shocked. 'Soph's kind of right! The diamonds were never stolen in the first place! April hid them in her bag and made the whole thing up to get Polly in trouble. Polly told Nan she thought she was being framed – she just didn't realise that it was April who was doing the framing!'

'I knew it was a set-up!' cried Nan happily. 'I've seen this kind of thing on *Murder, She Wrote*.'

'But why would April want to frame Polly?' Soph asked. 'She couldn't have known about Polly's secret feelings for James.'

'I was the only one Polly confided in,' Nan nodded.

I took a deep breath. 'Basically, Polly did nothing to provoke April. She always treated her with genuine respect. Polly thought April was lovely.'

Nan snorted. 'Framing your fiancé's friend for robbery is hardly the act of a lovely person!'

Suddenly, Abs's eyes glazed over. I could totally tell her massivo brain was about to come up with something genius. 'April must have taken the moisturiser from Polly's room,' Abs said. 'She told

Polly and James that she wanted to call Los Angeles after the Banana Splits' performance. But she wasn't on the phone, mes amis, she was planting the fake clues!'

'Then she hid the jewellery in her bag and screamed for help,' I finished.

'Exactamundo!' grinned Abs.

'Now all we need to do is establish a motive. Why did April do what she did?' said Nan.

Soph fiddled with April's diamonds, while we talked about the different possibilities.

'The stories in the papers must have been too much for her,' Abs said thoughtfully. 'Let's face it, April was on a one-way plane to Jealousville.'

'Jealousville? Is that in America?' Nan asked.

Suddenly my phone beeped.

'It's a text from Mum,' I said.

Mum: I've just been to check your room. Where are you all?

Me: Down the hall in Nan's room. :-)

Mum: What are you up to?

I groaned, and showed the phone to Nan. 'Mum's asking questions. What shall I say? We weren't supposed to be getting involved, remember? We promised.'

'Don't worry, love,' said Nan. 'I'll deal with your mother.'

I handed my phone over to Nan and tried to explain how to text.

'Keep pressing the key until you get the word you want,' I told her.

'And then press this button to send the text,' Abs added helpfully.

Nan's face lit up as the letters appeared on the screen. 'This is better than Morse code,' she beamed. 'Ooh, talking of police, you ought to ask the hotel to call them in, Rosie.'

'When were we talking of police?' I asked, wondering if I'd missed something.

'Morse code. Inspector Morse. He's in the police,' Nan explained slowly.

Oh, silly me.

'Hey, once we've handed over the diamonds,

Polly will be off the hook!' smiled Abs. 'We've done it! We've solved the mystery!'

'Er, there's just one teeny problem,' Soph said, slowly raising her hand.

We all looked. April's ring was totally wedged on Soph's finger.

'It's a tiny bit stuck,' Soph whispered miserably.

'Sacrebleu, Sophie!' I cried. 'Why on earth did you do that?'

'I just wanted to know what it would feel like to wear such a fabby ring,' Soph replied.

'Well, judging by the way your finger is turning blue, I'd say it feels pretty tight!' said Abs.

'I can't get it off,' squeaked Soph, looking a bit panicky.

'You're going to have to marry James, then,' I grinned. 'Lucky you.'

'Ooh, but my finger really hurts!' Soph wailed, not seeing the funny side at all.

Me and Abs stopped mucking about and tried to help. First I held Soph's hand steady while Abs pulled the ring, then I pulled the ring while

Abs held her hand.

'It's not working!' cried Soph.

'Try soap and water,' suggested Nan, her eyes still glued to my phone.

We raced into the bathroom and squirted loads of liquid soap on Soph's hand.

'Try to twist it,' said Abs.

Soph wiggled the ring. 'You try, Rosie.'

I gripped the ring and pulled. Soph stumbled towards me. 'Hold on to her, Abs!' I cried.

Abs grabbed Soph around the waist and I pulled again. Suddenly it gave way. I flew backwards and crashed into the bath. The soapy ring pinged out of my hand and flew into the air.

'Nooooo!' screamed Abs, as the ring curved up in a graceful arc and plummeted down the loo with a splash.

Soph pulled me out of the bath and we peered into the toilet.

'I can see it,' said Abs.

'Then you'd better get it,' Soph told her.

'No way, José! *You* get it!' cried Abs.

'You,' said Soph, digging her in the ribs.

'I'm not putting my hand in there. You do it,' Abs insisted.

Soph suddenly looked at me. 'Rosie, you dropped it. You should get it.'

I shook my head. 'Er, hello? *I* just saved your finger from turning blue. It's totally *your* fault the ring is down the loo!'

'Come on, Soph, you know what to do,' giggled Abs.

Soph rolled up the sleeve of her cardigan and gave us a pleading look.

'In you go, Little Mermaid,' I told her.

She plunged her arm into the toilet, making an awful face as she groped around.

'Ew!' screamed me and Abs.

'Ew! Ew! Ew!' wailed Soph, pulling her dripping hand out.

'Have you got it?' I asked, clutching Abs in horror.

'Voilà, mes amis,' said Soph, holding up the ring.

I looked at it suspiciously. 'You'd better wash that before I give it to the police.'

* * *

I left the girls and Nan mopping up the bathroom and set off towards the lift with the diamonds in my pocket. I had it all worked out. Reception would call the hotel manager and she'd call in the police. I stood by the lift and imagined Polly's grateful smile. She would be sooo relieved when she found out we'd cleared her name!

Suddenly, the lift doors opened and my smile faded. April was standing right there in the lift! Quelle horreur!

She stepped into the hall and started walking menacingly towards me. 'Where are my diamonds?' she hissed.

I took a few steps backwards. 'I don't know what you're talking about!'

April glared at me. 'Oh, don't play the innocent with me, little missy. I saw you and your friends picking up my jewellery in the street.'

My hand went automatically to my pocket. 'I don't know anything about diamonds, but can I have your autograph, please?' I said, desperately trying to blag my way out.

A cold grin spread across April's face. 'If you don't know anything about my diamonds, why are you so worried about what's in your pocket?'

For a split second we stood there staring at each other, then I turned on my heel and sprinted towards Nan's room. I should have acted faster. April had no trouble catching me up and cutting me off. She forced me to turn and then she chased me in the opposite direction.

I looked wildly around for an escape route. I couldn't get back to Nan's room. I couldn't get to the stairs. I was totally trapped! *Think, Rosie, think!* Suddenly, I remembered the emergency-exit map on the back of the bedroom doors. That was it! There was an emergency stairwell that ran through the centre of the hotel! It was my only chance! I pounded towards the end of the hall and wrenched open the grey emergency-exit door. OK, so it wasn't exactly a classic emergency scenario, like a fire or a flood, but being chased by the loonissimo fiancée of a famous celeb had to count for something! I ran across the short hallway and started pelting down the dimly lit stairs.

I could hear April's footsteps racing right behind me. Then her hand was on my shoulder. I screamed desperately for help and pulled away, my thoughts jumbled as my feet flew down the stairs. I had to get out. I had to get the police. I had to . . . Suddenly my foot caught on something and my legs tangled beneath me. I cried out in alarm and tried to grab the rail but it was too late – I was already falling.

'Give me my diamonds!' April called, somewhere behind me.

Everything started to blur as I hurtled down the stairs, bumping against the walls as I fell. I flung my arms out, trying to grab on to something, anything, but it was no good. Suddenly I heard a sickening crack, a bolt of pain shot through my head, and my world went black.

Chapter Seven

I opened my eyes slowly. What were those fuzzy
shapes, swaying around in front of me? I squinted
at them suspiciously. Wait a second! They weren't
shapes! They were people! I closed my eyes again.
Why were people staring at me? Maybe I was
dreaming . . .

I opened one eye and had another look. Nope,
they were definitely real people. I opened the
other eye and tried to make out their faces,
recognising Soph, Abs, Mum, Nan, James . . .
James? What the crusty old grandads was James

Piper doing in my bedroom?!

I sat bolt upright and stared around me. Hang on, if this was my bedroom, then where were my *Fusion* posters? And my wardrobe? I looked across at James, who was sitting at the end of my bed. Wasn't there usually a pile of old clothes where he was sitting? And why were Abs and Soph clutching each other and crying?

'What's going on?' I said in a quivery voice.

'Rosie, you're in hospital,' Mum said softly. 'You had a bit of a fall and you've bumped your head. It's nothing to worry about, sweetie, but you have been unconscious for a few hours.'

I blinked at her. A few *hours*? Seriously? I turned my head and looked at James again. He raised an eyebrow and winked. Sacrebleu! I looked at Abs and Soph, who beamed back, sniffing happily. Then Nan gave me a little wave and nodded reassuringly. Everyone was being very nice all of a sudden.

Then I got the uncomfortable feeling that a bit of my hair was sticking up at a right angle, the way it always does in the morning. I put my hand up to my head and raked my fingers through my hair, keeping well clear of the back of my head, which hurt. OK, so I was in not-exactly-glamorous hospital, but there was still a real live film star at the end of my bed.

I closed my eyes again, trying to piece together what had happened, but my memory was too hazy. Mum squeezed my hand.

'What happened to me?' I asked.

'We're not really sure, honey. James found you unconscious at the bottom of the emergency-exit stairs.'

'I've been using the emergency staircase to avoid the crowd in the lobby,' James explained.

Suddenly I remembered pushing open a grey door and running down the emergency stairs. But why was I running? What was the emergency? I put my hand up to the back of my head and gingerly felt the bump on my skull. It was huge, like one of those bumps that cartoon characters get after they've been bashed with a hammer. My face felt all sore too.

Wait a second. What was I doing wearing this gown thing? Where were my clothes? And, more to the point, what had I been wearing when James found me? Sacrebleu, what if I'd been wearing a skirt?! What if I'd actually passed out with my skirt over my head and James had found me with my knickers on show – right there at the bottom of the stairs for all to see? QUELLE HORREUR!

I felt my face go red as I frantically looked around the ward. When I spotted my jeans and T-shirt on a chair near the bed, I let out a sigh of relief.

Abs pushed a wheelie tray-table out of the way and stepped towards me. She tipped her head to the side and raised her eyebrows. Somehow I knew that she was asking me if I was OK. I met her eyes and tried to communicate my skirt-and-knicker panic by the powers of telepathy.

She gave me a funny look. 'Do you want a glass of water or something, Rosie?'

Hmmm. Obviously the bump on my head

hadn't done anything to increase my telepathic powers.

'The doctor said that you're going to have two black eyes tomorrow,' Soph told me, as Abs poured some water. 'But don't worry, amigo, the goth look is coming back in, so you'll be totally fashion-forward!'

I looked at Soph and a picture of her struggling to pull off a sparkly ring popped into my head. A diamond ring. April's ring! Zut alors! It was all flooding back to me. We'd found the jewellery that Polly was accused of stealing and April had tried to get it back . . . that's why I was running. That's why I fell!!!

I swung my legs out of bed and tried to get up. 'Have you called the police?' I asked Nan urgently.

'Now, now, dear, there's no need to panic. Get back into bed. That's my girl,' said Nan, gently lifting my legs back on to the mattress.

'Have you called the police? I repeated, as Mum tucked the sheets around me like I was about seven.

'We haven't had a chance to, love. We've all been too busy worrying about you,' Nan replied.

'Why would you want to call the cops?' James asked in his sexy American drawl.

Despite the massivo emergency situation, I couldn't help totally loving the way he made everything sound like a line from a film.

'It was an accident, right?' James continued. 'So you guys report accidents to the cops? Boy, things are different in England.' He tapped his toe on the floor and shrugged.

It was about then that I noticed that everyone was looking at James a bit shiftily. Duh, of course! He had no idea about April's involvement in my accident or in the whole framing-Polly-for-a-crime-she-didn't-commit scenario! He was clueless. Come to think of it, I hadn't actually told anybody about April causing me to fall, so *everyone* was clueless, in a way.

'Do you remember what happened, love?' Nan asked gently.

Suddenly I felt weak. I pulled myself up to a

sitting position and looked around the room. 'After I left Nan's room, I went to catch the lift down to the lobby.'

Five heads nodded around me. 'Go on,' Soph said encouragingly.

'But when the lift arrived, April was in it. She started chasing me so I made for the emergency exit and ran for help. That's when I fell . . .'

'What in the name of Texas?' exclaimed James. I looked up and saw his bewildered face. 'What has April got to do with this?' he asked. 'She wasn't even in the hotel. We had a bit of a fight and – well, she was upset. She went for a walk. How could she have been chasing you, kid? She has nothing to do with it!'

Er, excusez-moi, Mr James Piper, but your fiancée has everything to do with it! I shrugged helplessly at Abs and Soph. What could I say? How were we going to get James to believe us?

Suddenly, we heard footsteps clip-clopping over the tiled floor. The curtains around my bed flew open and April stood there, glaring at me. There were two policemen by her side. And they were HUGE.

April turned to James, her evil glare melting into a sugary smile.

'James, darling, I've got something to tell you,' she said in a silky voice.

I stared at Soph and Abs and they stared back, eyes huge. Was April going to confess her crimes? I watched her intently, half-expecting some kind of dramatic breakdown, but instead of admitting the error of her ways, she walked calmly to the corner of the cubicle and whipped my jeans off the chair.

I jumped out of bed in a panic. The diamonds! They were in the pocket of my jeans! Suddenly, I felt a weird breeze against my bum. The dodgy blue gown had a huge-issimo split up the back! Sacrebleu! Had I just flashed my bum at a famous film star?

I grabbed the two bits of material, frantically yanking them together. Then I looked helplessly at April. There was nothing I could do. She was already pulling the diamond necklace and engagement ring out of my pocket. I shot a look at James, who was gazing at me with disappointment and shock.

'This isn't what it looks like!' I cried desperately. 'I'm not the thief!'

April let out a silvery laugh. 'This is exactly what it looks like! Arrest that girl.' she snapped at the policemen. 'She's the one who stole my diamonds! She's had them all along.'

Chapter Eight

There was a three-second pause, then everyone started yelling at once. Mum and Nan yelled at April, April yelled at Soph and Abs, and the policemen yelled at everyone. I stood by my bed in my dodgy hospital gown and burst into tears. It was très stressful.

April threw me a scornful look as I let out a huge-issimo sob. 'Cry all you like! You're still going to jail!' she screamed menacingly.

I backed away, crashing into the wheelie tray-table and knocking it sideways. It shot off like a torpedo, hurtling towards the wall at lightning speed.

'MY DAUGHTER IS NOT GOING ANY-WHERE,' shouted Mum, grabbing my arm.

Soph and Abs screamed as the table rebounded off the wall and freewheeled back towards us. They leapt out of the way as it flew past, then flung themselves between me and April like a human shield.

'Rosie's staying right here!' yelled Soph, looking totally menacing despite her mega-fluffy hairclips.

There was a loud crash as the table keeled over with its wheels still spinning madly.

'SHE'S A THIEF!' shouted April above the whirring of the wheels.

'If Rosie's a thief, then I'm a custard cream!' Nan yelled passionately. She jumped over the fallen table and launched herself at April. 'TAKE THAT!' she cried, slapping April energetically with her handbag.

'Ouch!' whined April.

'HI-YAAAAAAAA!' screeched Nan, whacking

April again. I stopped crying and gawped in amazement. She was a total black belt in bag-slapping!

'Help me! She's got a brick in her bag!' April wailed to the policemen.

'How dare you! It's not a brick [*whack*] it's the manuscript of the murder-mystery book I'm [*whack*] writing!' cried Nan.

One of the gigantic policemen marched over to Nan and hoisted her on to his muscly shoulders.

'You put me down this instant!' cried Nan, kicking her legs around in the air.

Suddenly, James stood up. 'IN THE NAME OF TEXAS, WOULD Y'ALL JUST SHUT UP!'

I sniffed loudly. Oh, la, la, James was totally gorgey when he was angry!

The policeman put Nan back on the ground and she brushed herself off in a dignified manner. 'Well!' she bristled, 'that was *most* uncalled for!'

Abs shot me a look and winked at me. 'Your nan is a star!' she mouthed.

'You *all* are!' I mouthed back, my heart still

pounding under my hospital gown.

'Right, is somebody going to tell me what's going on?' James looked from me to April. 'What this all about, honey?' he asked.

'Well, me, Soph and Abs saw April –'

'Since when have *you* been his honey?' April said crisply.

'Er – um,' I stammered, going as red as a bottle of ketchup.

'Don't worry, Rosie dear. I'll sort out this nonsense.' Nan squared her shoulders and looked James in the eye. 'These three girls may look like ordinary teenagers but they've solved more crimes than she's had hot dinners!' Nan jabbed a disapproving finger in April's direction. 'They recovered the diamonds after they'd been dropped in the street.' Nan paused and looked at James dramatically, waiting for a response.

James leaned towards her. 'But who dropped them?'

Nan nodded smartly toward April. '*She* did!'

'That's not true!' April exploded. 'Rosie had

the diamonds. She's the thief! The jewellery was in her pocket – what more evidence do you people need?'

'Then what about Polly?' Abs asked calmly. 'You told James that *she* was the thief!'

I wiped my tears and exchanged a meaningful look with Soph. Something told me Abs was about to unleash her super-sized brainpower.

April stared at Abs and faltered for a second. 'She . . . they . . . they were in it together!' she cried.

'Right,' said Abs, 'so they were in it together, and Rosie smeared Polly's moisturiser around your room.'

'Yes,' said April uncertainly.

'And why would she do that?' Abs probed. 'If Rosie and Polly were working together, like you said, why would Rosie slosh a whole load of Polly's face cream around?'

'I don't know how the minds of criminals work!' April cried, looking beseechingly at James.

'Oh, but I think you do,' Abs said softly.

James shifted from one foot to the other.

'These people are mad! This whole country is mad! I want to go back to America!' cried April, flinging herself into his arms.

'I think we'd better continue this down at the station,' said one of the policemen. 'If you'd all follow me, please, we've got some cars waiting outside.'

There was a sudden flash of white, and a tiny woman dressed in a medical coat appeared next to the towering policemen.

'I am Dr Alison King,' she announced. 'And in no way are you to disturb my patient. Miss Parker has had quite a bad bump to the head and we want to keep her in overnight for observation. She's been unconscious for hours. She needs total rest now.' She gestured meaningfully towards the overturned table. 'I think she has had more than enough excitement for one day.' She opened her mouth to continue her lecture, then spotted James.

'Hi!' said James, noticing the doctor's mesmerised stare. Let's face it, it wasn't exactly hard to miss. I mean, if she'd stared any more, her eyes would have actually fallen out of her head and rolled around on the floor like marbles.

'Oh gosh!' said Dr King, straightening her stethoscope and batting her eyelashes. 'May I have your autograph?' She handed James my medical chart and a pen.

'Don't you guys need this?' James said uncertainly, waggling the chart at her.

'Oh, no. It's not important,' said Dr King.

Eh? Not important? How could she say my medical chart was not important? She'd just said I'd been unconscious for hours! How much more important could it get? I mean, my brain could have had a serious dent in it! And I might be going to prison! I was going to prison with a denty brain and all Dr King could do was ask for autographs!

I was just about to object strongly about my chart, and my head, and prison and everything, when the policemen gruffly announced that they still wanted to question everybody else down at the station. Mum tried to point out that she didn't want to leave me alone, as I was only 14, but they weren't having any of it. They had their questions and that was that.

The police waited by the door while we said goodbye. Mum and Nan hugged and kissed me, then Soph and Abs practically squeezed me in half.

'We'll text you!' Soph whispered next to my ear.

Nan picked up the wheelie table and put a packet of bourbons and my mobile on the top.

'Don't worry, ma soeur. We'll get you out of this mess,' Abs promised, hugging me tight.

'Try to get some rest,' said Mum, looking upset.

I nodded at them all, holding back my tears as they filed out of the room. April and the policemen followed but James hovered by the door for a second. Our eyes locked. He took a breath to say something. My heart jumped. Was he going to tell me that he believed me? Was he going to tell me that he knew I didn't steal April's diamonds? But instead of speaking, James just tipped his head in a nod and slipped out of the door.

About an hour later, I was lying in my hospital bed staring at the ceiling and panicking about going to prison. Suddenly, my mobile beeped.

Soph: At the police stn. Ur mum being questioned now. April in other room. Ur nan is force-feeding us biscuits. Abs has eaten TEN!

Me: But what's happening? Hv u been questioned yet?

Soph: We r still waiting. They are talking to April and your mum. Sooo tired. It's past midnight!

Me: I kno. Can't sleep tho.

Soph: How's your head?

Me: Feels OK. James gave me such a weirdissimo look earlier.

Just then, a nurse came into the room and shook her head at me. 'I'm afraid mobile phones are banned in this hospital,' she told me.

'But I just need to –' I started.

'I'm sorry, Rosie. Rules are rules. Anyway, it's ever so late now. You need plenty of rest. Try to settle down.' She gently took the phone out of my hands and plumped up my pillows.

I flopped back on them with a sigh. This was going to be the longest night of my life.

* * *

'Wake up, Rosie, there's a visitor here to see you,' said the nurse. 'Visiting doesn't start until eleven, but in your case we've made a special exception.'

I nodded miserably and rubbed my eyes. I suppose hospitals do have to make special exceptions when the police turn up to arrest a patient. I mean, if they thought you were a hardened criminal, they wouldn't just leave you to wander around in your bum-flashing hospital gown, would they?

I glanced over at my jeans and T-shirt and wondered if the police would let me change before they arrested me. I mean, being arrested for a crime you didn't commit is bad enough, but being arrested for a crime you didn't commit whilst sporting a bum-flashing nightie would be très hideous. Hang on though – maybe the police would want me to change into some kind of prison outfit to save time.

I felt a single tear drip down my cheek. Seriously, I would actually rather be on holiday with Amanda Dork-Hawkins in Jersey than be facing arrest in a bumless gown.

The curtains around my bed opened and I braced myself.

How weird. Instead of sending in the gigantic policemen, the police force had sent in a huge bunch of flowers. I stared at them. They were being carried by a plain-clothes detective. And, OK, she was wearing totally nice shoes, but she was probably the toughest detective they had.

'Hello, Rosie,' said the detective, lowering the flowers.

I gasped happily. It wasn't a detective, it was Polly McAllistair! I jumped out of bed, holding my gown at the back, and gave her a one-armed hug.

'I've got news,' Polly said, excitedly. 'The Hotel Kesterton have CCTV footage of what happened last night. The police have watched everything. April chasing you. You falling. Everything!'

'Sacrebleu!' I sighed, plonking myself down on the bed.

'That's not all,' Polly continued. 'There was even footage of April trying to get at the diamonds out of your pocket. But something must have disturbed her, because suddenly it shows her stepping over your unconscious body at the bottom of the stairs. She walked away as if you weren't even there! The police have all the proof they need. My name is cleared and it's thanks to your bravery!' She sat next to me and took my hand. 'Thank you, Rosie.'

I could feel all the worry and stress draining out of my body like water going down a plughole. Everything was going to be OK! We were in the clear! I sooo wasn't going to prison! And neither was Polly!

'Why did April do it, do you think?' I said, after a minute.

Polly shook her head. 'I don't know, Rosie.'

Just then, a man in a white coat popped his head around the curtains.

'Hi. I'm Dr Holt, one of the consultants,' he said. 'Miss McAllistair, it's a pleasure to have you here, but I'm afraid Rosie needs her rest.'

'Of course,' Polly smiled. She squeezed my hand and got up to leave.

'Oh, er, just one thing,' said the consultant. 'I don't suppose I could have your autograph?'

Chapter Nine

I woke up a few hours later, feeling about a million times better. I was just wondering if I could creep outside to phone the girls when Dr King appeared by my bed. I gawped at her in surprise. She was wearing full make-up. And when I say full, I mean f-u-l-l! There was more lip gloss on her than the whole of Girls Aloud wear on a night out. And her eye make-up? Don't get me started!

OK, so I'm not exactly a make-up expert, but Soph has given me a lot of tips. She's even invented her own golden rules.

Soph's golden rules of make-up application:

1. Less is more, so always be subtle. (Take note, Dr Alison King!)
2. Make-up should be expressive and send a message to the world. Just make sure your message isn't, 'Hi there! I'm starring in a pantomime!'
3. Don't be afraid of colour, unless it's afraid of you. (I have to say that I've never really understood this one. But Soph is always repeating it, so it must mean something . . .)

Anyway, it didn't exactly take a genius to work out Dr King's message to the world – she practically had 'I Love James Piper' stamped on her head!

'Hello, Rosie! Is James here today?' she beamed.

I was just about to open my mouth when Dr Holt jogged on to the ward and skidded across the floor tiles. 'Am I too late?' he gasped, panting like a marathon runner. 'Have I missed her?'

'Rosie is right here, as you can see,' said Dr King, looking confused.

'No, not Rosie – Polly! Polly McAllistair! The nurses told me she was here!' puffed Dr Holt.

'What? Was James with her?' cried Dr King. 'Have we missed them both?'

I rolled my eyes. Aaarrrrgggghhh! *Seriously, like what is up with these people?*

'I expect they'll both be back in tomorrow, eh, Rosie?' smiled Dr Holt.

'But can't I go back to the hotel today?' I asked quickly.

'No, no. Not yet!' said Dr King with a hint of panic in her voice.

'We'd like to keep you in for . . . er . . . observation,' said Dr Holt.

'Observation! Absolutely!' nodded Dr King with enthusiasm. 'Now, do all your friends know when visiting hours are?'

'We could always give James and Polly a call if you want to let them know,' said Dr Holt with a helpful smile.

A few minutes later, I put my coat over my hospital gown and slipped out with my phone in my pocket. I was dying to tell the girls what Polly had said. As soon as I got into the car park, I took out my phone to call Abs, but I couldn't get through, so I sent her a text:

I'M A CELEBRITY SLEUTH, GET ME OUT OF HERE!!!

I grinned to myself and waited for my phone to beep.

Suddenly, I heard a yell. 'Rosie! What are you doing out here in the cold?' It was Mum. She was belting across the car park, looking very unimpressed to see me wandering about in my coat-gown combo.

'Um, I just wanted to send a text,' I said, hugging her tight and smiling at Nan, Abs and Soph over her shoulder.

'You should be inside, in the warm,' Mum told me, steering me back through the automatic doors.

'We've got news!' Abs said, as we walked back to the ward.

'Yes, we've got so much to tell you,' said Nan, beaming happily as she spotted her unopened biscuits on my wheelie table. 'Ooh. I'll open these for you, love. You've got to keep your strength up.'

'Never mind the biscuits! I cried. 'Tell me what's been going on!'

'Well, you know the biggest news because Polly told you,' said Soph.

I nodded. 'She came in très early.'

'She was dying to tell you about the CCTV herself and wanted to thank you in person,' Soph smiled. 'We saw her this morning at breakfast.'

'But anyway, after we saw Polly, we bumped into James,' Abs said. 'You know how he looked in that film when he played the part of a man who never slept?

'*The Insomniac*,' I nodded.

'Yeah. He looked like that.' Abs said gravely.

'Sacrebleu!' I cried, picturing James's haggard face and bloodshot eyes in the film.

'Oui,' said Soph, shaking her head. 'Très, très pas bon.'

'Poor young man!' Nan said, crunching into a biscuit.

'He told us that he couldn't help feeling responsible for what had happened to you and Polly,' said Mum.

'That's crazy!' I cried. 'It wasn't his fault! It was all April!'

Mum tucked the covers around me. 'Don't worry, sweetheart. We told him you'd feel that way.'

'He wanted us to pass on his very best wishes,' Nan told me, with an exaggerated wink.

I have to say, it was a huge-issimo relief that James knew I wasn't the thief. I mean, it's pretty hideous when a top film star thinks you swiped his fiancée's diamonds.

There was the sound of footsteps. 'Another visitor for you, Rosie,' said a nurse, leaning around the curtain.

We all turned and stared, wondering who it could be.

It was James. Abs was totally right, he did look très terrible, but he also looked très attractive in an action-hero kind of way.

After a while, I realised I was totally staring at him. Actually, we kind of all were. I quickly pulled my eyes away and started looking at my nails. Nan gave a little cough and the girls shuffled about on the floor.

Mum recovered first. 'Come in, James. We were just passing on your best wishes to Rosie.'

'Um . . . er . . . thank you,' I said witlessly.

'No, it is *I* who should thank *you*,' said James in a posh English accent. He bowed at me as if we were in a costume drama, and we all laughed. His emotional ordeal clearly hadn't damaged his acting skills or his fabuloso sense of humour.

Suddenly, James's smile faded and I could see that, despite the joking around, his eyes were full of sorrow.

'How are you doing?' I asked quietly, as he settled himself on a chair.

'Not so bad,' he nodded. 'I'm sorry to interrupt

your time with your friends and family, but I just wanted to come and explain, Rosie. I owe you so much. All of you.' He gestured around the room to Abs, Soph, Mum and Nan. 'If you hadn't stepped in, my good friend Polly would have been convicted of robbery, and I would have married April, never knowing what she was truly like.' He paused and looked at his hands.

'But none of this was your fault!' I said quickly.

'Thank you. That means so much. You know, I keep going over and over all the events in my mind and I just can't understand how I missed the signs. But when you love someone . . .'

'It's hard, I know,' said Mum wisely.

James nodded. 'I thought April was the love of my life. When my brother had his car accident last year, April was one of his nurses. When my hope for David had almost gone, it was April who made me believe that he would get better. She gave me support through the darkest days of my life. Then when David started making a recovery, I was just so happy and grateful to her. All I could see was her kindness and generosity, and I fell in love.'

'That sounds totally romantic,' sighed Soph.

'It was,' said James with a wistful smile. 'As soon as David was better, we all went to stay at my parents' farm back in Texas. One night, after a big family meal, I realised I wanted to spend my life with April, so we got engaged there and then. Perhaps it was too soon, but you know what it's like when you're in love.'

Nan nodded knowingly and I stared at her in alarm. 'Your grandad was a very dashing man,' she explained, catching my eye.

'After a few months, things started going wrong,' continued James. 'I was playing the lead in an action film and April became very stressed and jealous. She gave up her job and followed me everywhere I went. At one point, we had to film in the Sahara desert and Antarctica in the space of three weeks. It was a gruelling amount of travelling, but April insisted on coming. At first, I thought it was because she wanted to be with me, but then I realised that she didn't trust me with the lead actress. She threw tantrums whenever we filmed romantic scenes – it was awful. Things got even worse when we came to London for the play. April knew Polly and I were old friends and the silly rumours about us in the papers made her even more jealous. Then, a few days before the robbery, she suddenly seemed to calm down. I thought that she was finally getting over her insecurities, but I was wrong. She was planning to frame Polly! April wanted Polly out of the play and out of my life and she was prepared to break the law to get what she wanted.'

James turned to me, his eyes brimming with tears. 'Rosie, the April I fell in love with would never walk away from somebody who was hurt. When I saw her stepping away from your unconscious body on the CCTV footage, I knew she wasn't the person I'd thought she was – the person I'd fallen in love with.'

The curtains around my bed parted and Polly slipped in. She stood behind James's chair and patted his shoulder comfortingly. He looked up at her and smiled broadly.

'I brought the tickets you asked for,' she said, handing a sheaf of tickets to James.

'These are for all of you,' he smiled, giving the tickets to Mum. 'We want you all to be there on the opening night of our play. It would mean a lot to us to have you in the audience. Promise me you'll come.'

※ ※ ※

A few days later, we were waiting in the hotel lobby for our cab.

'How's your head, Rosie?' asked Mum, for about the thousandth time.

'Mum, the hospital wouldn't have let me out if they thought it might fall off!' I giggled, peering at my black eyes in Soph's make-up mirror. They weren't really black any more, but sort of yellow with greeny bits. I have to admit, it wasn't exactly surprising that Mum was a tad worried.

Just then, Polly and James came past on their

way to the theatre. 'We've got to rush off but Polly wanted to see you first,' James said with a smile.

'I thought these would look fabulous with your dress,' Polly said, slipping her shades over my bruised eyes.

Soph held up her mirror so I could have a look. Polly was right! The midnight-blue frames totally matched my dress!

'Thanks, Polly,' I said happily.

'Don't mention it!' Polly smiled.

'See you later, guys!' said James.

* * *

The play was a huge-issimo success. When it was over, we jumped to our feet and clapped until our hands were all tingly.

When the curtain finally went down, a totally gorgey bloke came over and spoke to Mum. 'James and Polly would like to invite you to the after-show party – it's being held at a secret location. Polly and James are waiting for you in their limo.'

Sacrebleu!

We whizzed through London in the back of the limo, chatting and laughing together.

'Get ready for the paparazzi,' James said as we arrived at the party venue.

Polly and James got out first. They stepped on to the red carpet and the crowd went totally wild! Cameras flashed. People cheered. It was loontastic!

When things had calmed down, we hopped out of the limo and started walking towards the door.

Suddenly, the cameras exploded into action again. I looked around, frantically trying to spot who the paparazzi were snapping.

'That's right, sweetheart. Give us an angle!' a photographer shouted in my direction.

'Hold the pose, please,' yelled another man with a camera.

'No way! They think you're famous, cos of Polly's sunglasses!' gasped Abs.

'Those shades totally give you star quality!' laughed Soph, as cameras flashed all around us.

I put my arms around my two best friends and we walked up the red carpet, blowing kisses to the paparazzi and giggling our heads off.

* * *

When we finally got inside, we were shown to a table. The waiter brought fruit-juice cocktails for me, Soph and Abs, and glasses of wine for Mum and Nan.

'Look, James is going to make a speech,' whispered Soph.

We looked at the raised platform where James was standing.

'It's good to see y'all,' he said in his Texan accent. 'It's been a difficult few days, and before we get this party started, I just wanted to thank some very important ladies. Rosie, Abs, Soph, Liz and Pam, I owe you all so much. Thank you from the bottom of my heart. And I also want to thank Polly McAllistair – a good friend and a great actress. Thanks for making the play so special, Polly!'

James walked over to where Polly was standing and pulled her up on to the platform. She blushed as he put his arm around her and gave her a little hug.

'You know what?' I said. 'I think this is what they call a happy ending.'

'Totally,' grinned Soph and Abs, as we clinked our glasses together.

Friendship Fun

Make every second with your bezzie count with these cool ideas!

Daydreamin' Divas

You probably spend loads of time chatting about things you'd love to do in the future, so pick one and make it happen. If your mate wants to be a fashion designer, then spend an afternoon making jewellery together. If you've always wanted a puppy, offer to dog-sit for a neighbour one weekend. Together, your dreams can come true!

Best Friends Forever

Never forget why you're bezzies! Sure, your friend might get on your nerves sometimes but there are good reasons why you two stick together through thick and thin. Try spending more time feeling smiley about her good points and less time being irritated by her bad habits and you'll become better friends than ever!

Pen Your Pal

If homework is taking over your life and your weekends are spent visiting your nan, then it can be tough to find time for your friend. Getting letters makes everyone feel special, so grab some notepaper and get scribbling. Funny stories and silly doodles are bound to brighten up her day!

Swap Till You Drop

Spending every Saturday shopping can get a bit pricey, so why not raid each other's wardrobes and have a swap-a-thon? Just exchanging a couple of T-shirts for a few weeks can lead to a total style re-vamp – and all for free! Sorted!

Get Gifty!

Making a personalised prezzie for your mate will make her grin! A photo collage or a memory-book filled with silly stories are two top ideas to get started on.

Fact File

NAME: James Piper

AGE: 31

STAR SIGN: Pisces

HAIR: Light brown

EYES: Brown

LOVES: Anything to do with the 1980s – it was a golden age!

HATES: Things not being quite as they seem

LAST SEEN: Dancing to his MP3 player with the volume up high in his dressing room

MOST LIKELY TO SAY: Come and join us for dinner – it's on me!

WORST CRINGE EVER: When he went into the ladies' loos in the hospital when his brother was ill. He walked straight into a group of blushing nurses who were sent into fits of giggles!

Megastar

Everyone has blushing blunders - here are some from your Megastar Mysteries friends!

Rosie

Me, Abs and Soph were going to a party and, for once, I decided to take Soph's advice and put a bit of effort into my appearance. I spent ages in the shower using all sorts of different lotions and potions and emerged feeling and smelling gorgeous. When I got round to drying my hair, something just wasn't right. It was completely stuck to my head and looked really strange. Eventually, I realised that I had forgotten to wash my conditioner out! I didn't have time to wash it again had to put it up to try to disguise how greasy it looked! I ended up going to the party looking like I hadn't washed my hair for a week – but at least I smelled nice!

Sophie

I spent weeks putting together a scrapbook for my art coursework. The topic was 'Me' and I'd filled the pages with scraps of gorgeous fabric, pictures of outfits from *Vogue* and loads of pictures from the amazing adventures Rosie, Abs and I have had together. I was so proud of it and thought I had really managed to sum up my life. On the day it was due, I grabbed it and ran to school and it was only as I handed it in that I noticed I had picked up the wrong book. It was the super-cringey baby album my mum had made for me when I was little! The whole class had a good laugh at pictures of me naked in the bath. Sooo blushsome – and hardly very artistic!

Cringes

Pam

I couldn't believe it when Abs told me she'd never tried banana custard, so I invited her and Soph round for Sunday lunch at our house. My custard looked lovely – it was a beautiful yellow colour and there wasn't a lump in sight. Everyone told Abs that she'd love it, and I couldn't wait to see the smile on her face when she tried it. But as soon as she put the first spoonful in her mouth, her face puckered up and she spat it out! I had a little try myself to see what was wrong and realised I'd poured in salt instead of sugar! It was *disgusting*! What a custard-y cringe!

Polly

A few years ago I was getting my hair done for a very glamorous award ceremony. My hairdresser was trimming when suddenly I sneezed. Her scissors cut right into my hair and left me with a tiny chunk of fringe about 2 centimetres long! It looked utterly ridiculous and we spend the rest of the afternoon trying out different ways of wearing hair clips, tiaras and scarves to cover up my tufty do. In the end, I had to make do with an Alice band, and I spent half the night patting my head to make sure that my sticky-up locks hadn't escaped. Crrringe!

Abs

Rosie, Soph and I decided that it was time to get fit, so we arranged to go swimming after school. When we got to the changing rooms, I pulled out what I thought was my costume, only to find that I had picked up my mum's by mistake! I decided I could handle wearing it, even though it didn't exactly look cool and was a few sizes too big. But when it got wet in the pool, the costume just got bigger and bigger until I looked like I was drowning in it! I hid in the water until it was time to leave, and when I got out of the pool it was practically round my knees! What a splashing shamer!

Are You a Megastar Myteries Super-fan??

Put your knowledge to the test with this fantastic quiz!

1
Rosie's favourite magazine is called Star Secrets
☑ True ☐ False

2
Liz Parker is mad about anything from the 1950s
☐ True ☑ False

3
Pam Parker hates watching murder-mystery programmes on TV
☐ True ☑ False

4
Rosie, Soph and Abs go to Whitney High School
☑ True ☐ False

5
Amanda Hawkins is always nice to Rosie, Soph and Abs
☐ True ☑ False

6
Rosie isn't really that interested in celebrities
☑ True ☑ False

Answers (no peeking!):

1. True 2. True 3. False 4. True 5. False 6. False 7. False 8. True 9. True 10. False

8/10 Jacob

7
Soph is brill at customising clothes
☑ True ☐ False

8
Rosie, Soph and Abs all live in Borehurst
☑ True ☐ False

9
Abs is a bit of a genius
● True ◐ False

10
Rosie thinks her mum's tribute band is really cool and not at all cringey
☐ True ☑ False

How many did you get right?

1–3 You're a Borehurst beginner
Did you even read this book?! Or maybe this was your first ever *Megastar Mysteries* read. Try getting your hands on some of the other books in the series and you'll learn all there is to know about Rosie and the gang in no time!

4–6 You're a Whitney High wannabe!
Hey, you know quite a lot about Rosie, Soph and Abs but you've still got a way to go. Maybe you were too busy working on solving your own mystery to really concentrate on this quiz!

7–10 You're a Megastar megastar!
You should be called Little Miss Mystery cos you're practically mates with Rosie, Soph and Abs! You're great a sniffing out a good mystery, and with everything you've learned from these ladies you're all set to solve it!

Soph's Style Tips

Make like a movie star with Sophie's hot Hollywood make over ideas!

SAY 'NO' TO LABELS!

Hollywood stars might be a bit obsessed with designer labels at times, but with the amazing selections of clothes available in charity shops and in the supermarket, why do they bother? Keep your eyes open and your pocket money could buy you designer style for pennies!

IT'S SUNNIES ALL THE TIME!

Never go anywhere without a pair of sunglasses – you might need to hide from people who've been fooled by your Hollywood makeover! And, once you've developed a superstar attitude to match, you may as well wear them indoors, too!

SPARKLE LIKE A STAR

If in doubt, get glittery! Don't be afraid to wear a shiny belt, sequinned cardigan or silver shoes with jeans and a simple top. It's an awesome look that makes you look like a real celebrity!

MESSY HAIR ROCKS!

Movie stars spend loads of money getting their hair styled to make it look like they've just got out of bed, but luckily it's a look that's not too hard to copy. As long as everything else about you looks fairly neat you should be able to avoid that dragged-through-a-hedge-backwards look!

Be a Dance Star
by Liz Parker

Use your space
The bigger your moves, the better. Work that stage!

Jazz hands
Spread your fingers and shake your hands like crazy. Remember, a huge grin sets off this move a treat

Shimmy
It's all in the shoulders. Wiggle them as fast as you can – it's brilliant!

Music Mad
There's only one thing to remember. The 1980s were a golden era. Try A-Ha, Duran Duran or my faves, Bananarama. OK, Girls Aloud are just about acceptable if you must move to something more modern . . .

Crazy Costumes
Colours
It's got to be bold, bright and baggy. Go for neon, if possible

Accessories
Never set foot on stage without legwarmers and sweatbands

Team style
Matching is best. For example, we Banana Splits members never go on stage without our matching yellow bandanas!

The Magic Touch
Teeth and eyes
Flash your pearly whites and smile with your eyes. Just not so much that you look like a loony though!

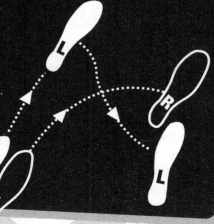

What's Your Reality Style?

Answer the questions to find out what kind of reality star you could be!

1. Are you mad about animals?

a. Yes, 100 per cent – pets are almost as good as mates!

b. I love watching programmes about them on TV, but animals are a lot of work to look after in real life

c. No, thanks! Cats are scratchy and dogs are smelly – what's to like?

2. Do you dream of being on telly?

a. Not really – I guess it would be OK but I'm not too bothered

b. Yes! All that pampering followed by fame and adoration sounds brilliant!

c. I don't care if it's on the stage, the sports ground or on TV – I just want to be famous!

3. Are you mobile mad?

a. Not really, I borrow my mum's sometimes but I'm not that bothered

b. I love my mobile – it's covered in stick-on gems and I change the ring tone every day!

c. I'm mad about texting and am the fastest texter ever!

4. How long does it take to do your hair in the morning?

a. I just brush and go and it usually looks fine!
b. Sometimes ages – a bad hair day would ruin my day!
c. I love trying out new styles for parties, but most of the time I just go for a simple ponytail

5. Have you got many pairs of shoes?

a. Just enough to have something for school, something for sport and something for parties – what more do you need?
b. A girl can never have too many pairs of shoes, right?
c. I've got quite a few, but I saw some amazing glittery ballet pumps the other day – better start saving!

How did you score?

Mostly As: Amazing Adventurer

You'd be right at home in a reality show set in an exotic location like an island or a jungle – and not just because your hair sometimes makes you look like you belong in the wild! You think that trying new foods and seeing cool creatures is really exciting cos you're a true daredevil at heart.

Mostly Bs: Hidden Camera Hero

Living in a house filled with celeb wannabes and hidden cameras would be brilliant for you! You're not shy and love to be surrounded by people, so what could be better than showing off twenty-four hours a day, seven days a week, with a brill bunch of new mates?

Mostly Cs: Stars in Your Eyes

You were born to perform so why not enter a TV talent show? You'd wow the judges with that gorgeous voice, gleaming smile and from-the-heart sob story! OK, so maybe that's a slight exaggeration, but at the very least you could win a moment of fame with a cringey audition!

Pam's Problem Page

Never fear, Pam's here to sort you out!

Dear Pam,

I don't want to sound mean, but my mum's driving me mad! She's obsessed with eighties pop music and loves nothing more than dancing round the lounge in some hideous skintight outfit, yodelling into her hairbrush. Why do I have to be stuck with the cringiest mum in the world?!

ROSIE

Pam says: Ooh, that's funny, your mum sounds just like my daughter, and I've got a granddaughter called Rosie, too — isn't that a strange coincidence? It sounds to me like your mum is bursting with talent and I think it's just lovely that she puts it to good use in your lounge. You should count yourself lucky to have such lively entertainment on offer, and I should keep your fingers crossed that you've inherited some of those singing and dancing skills! There's nothing like a good sing-song to lift the spirits — well, except a nice cuppa and a Bourbon biscuit, of course.

Can't wait for the next
book in the series?
Here's a sneak preview of

Runway

And don't forget to check out
www.mega-star.co.uk

Chapter One

I'm going to be totally honest. Me and football go together about as well as chocolate ice cream served with a topping of tomato ketchup. OK, so it might just have something to do with the fact that I'm rubbish at playing it. The last time I played at school I made a huge-issimo idiot of myself. We were outside and it was freezing. I'm not joking, it was so cold I was seriously in danger of having icicles form on my nose! Not only that, but it was totally wet and muddy from where it had been raining. We all stood around while teams were being picked, and as usual,

I was the last to get chosen. We started playing and I tried my best, I really did. Until Amanda Witch-face Hawkins – the nastiest girl in my year, no scratch that, make it the whole school – kicked the ball, aiming it straight at my face.

'Ouch,' I shouted, as the ball bounced off my nose. 'That hurt!'

Miss Osbourne blew her whistle and marched over.

'What's going on?' she demanded.

Amanda Hawkins smiled sweetly at her. 'I'm so sorry, Miss Osbourne,' she said. 'I accidentally hit Rosie in the face with the ball.'

'Yeah, right,' I muttered under my breath. 'If that was an accident I'm the next David Beckham.'

Miss Osbourne inspected my nose. 'It's not broken,' she said breezily. 'But

you may well have a big bruise.'

Great. Just great. Way to look good.

Miss Osbourne blew her whistle again. 'Resume play, girls!' she shouted, running up the pitch, totally oblivious to Amanda Hawkins grinning evilly and poking her tongue out at me.

After that, I soon gave up and just kind of hung around at the edge of the field. Miss Osbourne marched over.

'Rosie Parker!' she shouted. 'Start making an effort or you'll find yourself doing laps round the field in detention!' She put her hand on my back and tried to push me towards the pitch. But as the grass was so slippery, I lost my footing and ended up lying flat on my back in a big puddle of mud. Everyone stopped playing to look at me and immediately cracked up. Even Miss Osbourne was trying hard not to laugh and it was her fault I'd fallen over in the first place! To make matters even worse, when I stood back up I had mud all over the back of my tracksuit bottoms.

'Oh, look,' Amanda Hawkins sniggered. 'Dozy Rosie looks like she's pooed herself!'

OH HA DE HA DE HA! SOMEBODY CALL AN AMBULANCE! I MIGHT SPLIT MY SIDES FROM LAUGHING. HILARIOUS! I DON'T THINK.

Ten reasons why football is sooo NOT coolissimo:

1. Cos it gets you all muddy

2. Cos you have to wear seriously unflattering clothes and clodhopper boots

3. Cos you only get to dance when you score a goal

4. Cos you have to play it when it's seriously coldissimo outside!

5. Cos you always end up on the opposite team to your bestie

6. Cos those 90 minutes would be much better spent in the shops

7. Cos the boys never look as cute as David Beckham

8. Cos your hairstyle never survives a tackle from the opposition

9. Cos footy chants are just nowhere near as catchy as the latest chart hit

10. Cos a boring white ball is not as cool as a sparkly pink one!

So you can imagine I was seriously unimpressed when not only my whole school, but the whole town, suddenly went totally and utterly football crazissimo! And all because our town's local football team, Fleetwich United, had made it through to the knockout stages of the Nicholls Trophy Cup.

As me, Abs and Soph walked through the school gates, I did a double take.

'What the crusty old grandads?' I muttered, my mouth hanging open with shock.

Whitney High had been totally transformed. It was like a football fairy had visited it in the night. Even if you hadn't heard about Fleetwich's win, you wouldn't be able to miss it. There were yellow-and-black banners (Fleetwich United's colours) everywhere, all shouting the words 'Go! Fleetwich Go!'

The atmosphere was buzzing. Everywhere you looked boys were practising their best footy moves. And over to the far left, Amanda Hawkins and her cronies, Lara Neil and Keria Roberts were dressed in cheerleader outfits, throwing shapes.

'Morning, girls,' came a familiar voice.

I turned to see Mr Lord, our drama teacher, standing behind me. He'd swapped his usual multicoloured stripy scarf for a yellow and black one. He looked around him and gave a sigh of satisfaction.

'It's so great to see everyone so inspired,' he said, wistfully. 'You know, I'm thinking of writing a school play on football. You know, I could have been a footballer. One of the greats. Another David Beckham. But then I got the lead in the school play and could no longer go to practice. I sometimes wonder what might have been . . .' He trailed off.

'Oh, but football's loss was definitely drama's gain,' said Soph, smiling wickedly. 'I mean, where would *Doctor Who* have been without you?'

Mr Lord, as he never tires of telling us, was a Cyberman in the original series of *Doctor Who*. Seriously, the amount he goes on about it, you'd think he won an Oscar for it or something. As a result the whole school calls him Time Lord. But not to his face, obviously.

'So true,' said Time Lord, 'so true.' Smiling happily to himself, he wandered away.

Me, Soph and Abs cracked up. I was still laughing as I headed into registration. Mr Adams grinned at me,

'Nice to see you looking so happy, Rosie,' he said. 'I think we've all got cause for celebration today. Class, I'd like you to take a minute to reflect on the significance of United finally making it in the finals of the Nicholls Trophy Cup after twenty-six years of trying. I honestly never thought I'd live to see the day.'

I stared at him in horror. As teachers go, Mr Adams is pretty cool. And for someone so ancient – he's well into his thirties – he's totally good looking too. I've always thought he'd make a pretty good boyfriend for Mum. Up till now that is. I couldn't stand to live with a football freak. Talk about Yawnsville.

My phone vibrated in my pocket. Holding it under the table, so Mr Adams couldn't see, I had a sneaky peek . . .

Save me frm ftball madness! Can me &
Soph cme 2 yrs 2nte? Abs X

Checking Mr Adams wasn't watching, I quickly
texted back.

It's a plan, Stan!

'It's like the whole town's been possessed,' I
moaned that evening.

'*Tell* me about it!' Abs rolled her eyes. 'My dad's
so excited he's even entered Fleetwich FM's
competition to get Megan selected as the team
mascot. Honestly, I might think my little sister is a
complete utter brat, but even I wouldn't wish that
on her. He's driving Mum round the bend!'

'I just don't get it!' I sighed. 'Just because
Fleetwich United scraped a one–nil victory. I
mean what the crusty old grandads is all the fuss
about? The only thing that interests me are the
WAGs, especially Elizabeth Branscome.'

'Who?' asked Abs.

'You know,' I said, 'Elizabeth Branscome, the girlfriend of Ricardo Ferrara.'

'Who?' asked Abs.

'The one who scored the goal,' I explained. 'You must have heard of her. She's the most famous WAG on the planet.'

Abs looked totally bemused. 'Mes amis, I have no idea what you're talking about.'

That's Abs for you. She's a total brainbox, but her head is so full of equations and scientific facts it doesn't always have room for other stuff. I reached for my latest copy of *Star Secrets* – aka the best celebrity magazine in the world – and flicked though the pages until I found what I was looking for.

'Wives And Girlfriends,' I explained, shoving a feature on Elizabeth Branscome under Abs's nose. 'Usually of footballers,' I added, to make certain she'd got it.

'And Elizabeth's basically Queen WAG. Her clothes are to die for,' sighed Soph. 'Head to toe designer, but always with a twist. You can tell just by looking at her outfit, she's totally confident about how she looks and who she is. She's as beautiful on the inside as she is on the outside.'

This is something Soph's always done, checked out people's clothes and immediately been able to say what kind of person they are. As soon as she started at Whitney High, she had Amanda Hawkins pegged as a total witch. Seriously, it's a gift.

Abs started reading the feature. 'It says here that she wore three different ball gowns during one evening!' she said in disbelief.

'I know,' sighed Soph dreamily. 'Isn't she amazing?'

'But what does she actually *do*?' asked Abs.

Me and Soph looked at each other.

'I've absolutely no idea,' I said. 'I think she's just professionally gorgeous.' Abs rolled her eyes.

'Like that's a real job,' she said.

'Hey, it's a dirty job, but someone's got to do it,' said Soph. 'I'd swap places with her quicker than you can say haute couture!'

Abs opened her mouth to make a scathing comment, but fortunately at that moment Mum stuck her head round the door.

'Dinner's ready, girls,' she said, walking into the room. 'What do you think of my outfit?' she asked, giving us a quick twirl.

Have I mentioned that my mum's in an eighties tribute band called the Banana Splits? They're based on a girl band called Bananarama who, according to Mum, were the Girls Aloud of their day. Unfortunately, this means Mum also spends a lot of time in eighties outfits. Like the one she was busily modelling now.

As I stared in horror at her skin-tight catsuit that seemed to be made out of some multi-coloured stretch fabric and badly stitched-on lace, I couldn't help wishing she'd take a leaf out of Elizabeth Branscome's book. Honestly, I love my mum dearly, but sometimes I just can't help wishing she could be just a little bit more normal.